Classic Fairy Tales

BY CHARLES PERRAULT

ILLUSTRATED BY MICHAEL FIODOROV

VOLUME ONE

BARNES
&NOBLE
BOOKS
NEW YORK

Table of Contents

The Sleeping Beauty   5

The Fairies   23

Cinderella   29

Bluebeard   43

Hop O' My Thumb   53

Puss in Boots   77

Ricky-of-the-Tuft   87

Publisher's Note

It may be difficult to think of fairy tales and not have "Cinderella" and "Sleeping Beauty" come to mind. French writer Charles Perrault (1628-1703) published these among other stories in his *Tales of Mother Goose* in 1697. Perrault collected the tales, which were already known, and popularized them in print while adding his own storytelling touches. His "Cinderella" is the classic version known to most readers. His "Sleeping Beauty" and "Little Red Riding Hood" are perhaps better known in later Grimm versions (originally called "Brier Rose" and "Little Red-Cap" by the Brothers Grimm).

In classic fairy tale style, beautifully captured here by artist Michael Fiodorov, Perrault's heroes and heroines persevere to win their battles against ogres and other menacing enemies. Cleverness, intelligence, and goodness win the day. Has a bolder, more clever cat than Puss of "Puss in Boots" ever come along, or kinder, more patient protagonists than Cinderella or Prince Ricky of "Ricky-of-the-Tuft"? Good stories and memorable characters keep Perrault's tales inviting to modern readers!

The Sleeping Beauty

Once upon a time, there lived a king and a queen who had everything life could offer except a child. How fervently they wished for a baby to grace their lives. Then and only then, they knew, would true happiness come. Imagine their rejoicing when, at long last, the queen gave birth to a beautiful baby girl. The whole kingdom celebrated.

A great christening ceremony was held. The king and queen invited all the fairies they could find in the land (there were seven of them) to be godmothers for the princess. It was the custom of fairies at that time to give special talents or virtues to their godchildren. The king and queen hoped that, with the gifts of these seven godmothers, the princess would have all the perfections one could imagine.

After the christening, everyone returned to the palace. There a banquet had been prepared in honor of the fairies. At each fairy's place setting was a small box of solid gold. Inside were a spoon, fork, and knife made of gold and set with diamonds and rubies.

No sooner were they all seated than a very old fairy entered the room. No one had thought of inviting her because for fifty years she had not left her tower. Everyone believed that she was dead or under a spell. At once, the king ordered that a place be set for her at the table. But it was not possible to set out for her a solid gold box, as the other seven fairies had been given. Only seven gold boxes had been made.

The old fairy was greatly offended and began to mutter threats through clenched teeth. A younger fairy sitting nearby overheard her. Fearing that the old fairy might give the princess an evil gift, the young fairy quickly hid behind a curtain. She wanted to be the last to grant her gift, so that she might undo some of the harm that the old fairy surely planned.

The youngest fairy was the first to give her gift. She announced that the princess would be the most beautiful woman in the world. The second gave her a spirit as pure as a lamb. The third made her graceful. The fourth gave her the gift of dancing and the fifth, the gift of singing like a nightingale. The sixth gave her the ability to play any instrument.

Then came the old fairy's turn. Shaking from spite, she promised that the princess would prick her finger on a spindle, the wooden rod used in spinning to twist the thread. Then the princess would die.

Everyone shuddered. But at that moment the young fairy came from behind the curtain. In a clear, strong voice, she said, "Take heart, good king and queen, for your daughter will not die. Unhappily, I do not have the power to undo completely this evil spell that has been cast. Yes, the princess will prick her finger with a spindle. But instead of dying, she will merely fall into a deep sleep lasting a hundred years. At the end of that time, a prince will awaken her."

6

The king tried to prevent the disaster predicted by the old fairy. He immediately passed a law forbidding the use of spindles or owning of spindles.

Sixteen years passed. One day, when the king and queen had gone to one of their country homes, the young princess went wandering through the castle. She came at last to a tiny attic room at the top of the tower. There a skillful old woman sat spinning. The old woman rarely left her room and knew nothing of the law against spindles.

"What are you doing, good woman?" asked the princess.

"I am spinning, lovely child," replied the woman, who did not know the princess.

"Oh, how clever!" said the princess. "Let me try. I want to see if I can do it."

8

Perhaps what happened next happened because the princess was excited and a little confused. Perhaps it happened because of the old fairy's prophecy. But no sooner had the princess picked up the spindle than she pricked her finger. At once she fell unconscious.

The old woman, in a panic, called for help. People rushed in from all over the palace. They poured water over the princess's face, loosened her gown, slapped her hands, and even rubbed her temples with perfume. But nothing would awaken her.

In the middle of the confusion, the king and queen returned. They recalled the fairies' predictions and realized that this event had been bound to occur. They had the princess carried to the finest apartment in the palace. She was laid upon a bed with covers embroidered in gold and silver. The princess looked like a sleeping angel. Her enchanted sleep had not dimmed her natural color. Her cheeks were pink, and

her shiny lips were as red as coral. Her eyes were closed, but her steady breathing proved that she was alive. The king ordered that she be left to sleep.

When the accident befell the princess, the good fairy who had traded her death for a hundred-year sleep was twelve thousand leagues away. A dwarf wearing seven-league boots sped to her side to tell the news. (Such boots enable the wearer to cover seven leagues with every step.) The fairy immediately set off in her fiery chariot drawn by dragons. Within an hour, she arrived at the palace. The king himself helped her from the carriage and took her to view the sleeping princess.

The fairy approved of all that the king had done. Still, being more far-sighted than others, she realized that when the princess awoke, the girl would feel lost if she were alone in that old castle. So with her magic wand, the fairy touched everyone and everything in the castle, except the king and queen.

She touched officials, ladies-in-waiting, waiters, gentlemen, coachmen, scullery maids, fieldhands, guards, pages, and messenger boys. She touched the horses in the stable, the grooms, and the great guard dogs. She even touched little Puff, the princess's pet dog, who lay near her on her bed. The instant that she touched them, they fell asleep, not to be awakened until their young mistress awoke and needed them once more.

All was still. Even the spits over the fire, full of partridges and pheasants, fell asleep, as did the fire

itself. These events happened in an instant. Fairies work quickly.

Then the king and queen kissed their daughter and left the castle. They decreed that no one was allowed to enter the castle. The decree, however, was not needed, for within a quarter of an hour all about the castle grounds there sprang up trees, bushes, and prickly brambles. The forest was so thick that neither animal nor human could pass through. The only parts of the castle that could be seen were the turrets on the tops of the towers. Even those could be seen only from far off. The fairy did this so that nothing would disturb the sleeping princess.

A hundred years passed. The kingdom was now under the rule of a family different from that of the princess. The son of the present king was hunting not far from where the princess slept. He saw castle towers rising above the forest and asked what they were. Each of his men told the prince a different story, according to what he had heard.

Some of them said that it was an old haunted castle. Others said that all the witches of the land held their magic ceremonies there. The most common opinion was that an ogre lived there, and that he carried there the children that he managed to catch.

The prince did not know what to believe. Finally, an old peasant spoke up, "My good Prince, over fifty years ago, my dear father told me that in that castle is the most beautiful princess in the world. She must sleep for a hundred years. At the end of that time, she will be awakened by the son of a king. It is destined that they will be married."

12

Those words lit a fire in the prince's heart. He was sure that it fell to him to carry out this great adventure. Driven by a desire for love and glory, he decided in that instant to see the mysterious castle. As soon as he drew near the forest, the trees, the bushes, and the prickly brambles all moved aside to let him pass. He went straight toward the castle that he saw at the end of a great avenue. With surprise, he realized that not one of his servants had been able to follow him, for the forest had closed again as soon as he had passed. There was nothing, however, that could stop a young prince in love!

He came into a vast courtyard, and what a terrible silence there was! All around lay lifeless bodies

of people and animals. But the prince noticed the rosy
cheeks of the guards at the gates. He realized that they
were only asleep.

The prince walked through a great hall paved in
marble, climbed a grand staircase, and entered the
guardroom. The guards still stood in line, their pikes
on their shoulders, all snoring loudly. The prince
passed on through several rooms full of lords and
ladies, some standing, some sitting, all asleep.

Finally, he came to a gilded bedroom and found,
lying on a bed, the most beautiful vision he had ever
seen. It was the young princess, so radiantly beautiful
that she looked almost like a goddess.

Trembling, the prince approached her. He fell to

15

his knees next to her, admiring her. At that moment, the spell was broken, and the princess awoke. She looked at the prince with tenderness and he returned her gaze with a smile.

"Is it you, my lord?" she said. "I've waited so long for you!"

The prince was enchanted by these words and still more by the way they were said. He hardly knew how to show his own joy and gratitude. In simple words, he assured her that he loved her more than his own life.

He didn't speak elegantly, but this made his words even more pleasing to the princess. The prince was more ill at ease than she was—which was not surprising, considering that she had had such a long time to dream about what to say to him. For four hours they talked together, but still they told each other only half of what they had to say.

Meanwhile, the palace had awakened with the princess. Each person had begun at once to carry on with his or her work. Now, since not all of them were in love, most of them were dying of hunger! A lady-in-waiting, hungry like the others, grew impatient and told the princess that dinner was served. The prince helped the princess get up. She was already dressed magnificently. The prince guarded against telling her that her clothes were in a style his grandmother might have worn! This didn't make her any less pretty.

Together, they entered the hall of mirrors and dined there, served by the princess's personal staff. Violins and oboes played old-fashioned melodies that had not been heard for a hundred years.

After dinner, the prince and princess wasted no time and were married by the court chaplain.

Publisher's note: The second part of Perrault's Sleeping Beauty *is the lesser-known version of the tale. It is based on earlier stories and myths, and tells of the children born to the prince and princess and the struggle that ensues with the prince's mother.*

Early the next morning, the prince returned to his own city, knowing that his father would be anxious for news of him. He told his father that he had become lost while hunting in the forest. His father, the king, believed his son. His mother, however, was not convinced. She saw that he went out hunting each day and always had an excuse for staying away all night.

She realized that he had fallen in love, and she was not at all happy about it.

In fact, the prince lived with his princess in this manner for two whole years, and they had two children. The first was a daughter, named Aurora, which means "dawn." The second was a boy, called Sunshine, who was even more pleasing to look at than his sister.

To make her son confide in her, the queen often told him that he should marry. But the prince still kept his secret from her. Although he loved his mother, he didn't trust her because she came from a family of wealthy ogres. His father had married her for her money. It was whispered about court that she had an ogre's wicked nature and that, when she saw children passing by, she longed to pounce on them.

Two years later, when his father died, the prince became ruler of the kingdom. Then he publicly proclaimed his marriage. With great pomp, the new king brought his happy family to the kingdom.

A short time later, the king had to go away to war against a neighboring emperor, and it seemed that he would be away all summer. He left the management of the kingdom to his mother, the queen, urging her strongly to take good care of his wife and children. As soon as he had left, the queen-mother sent her daughter-in-law and grandchildren to a country house in the forest. There she planned to act upon her horrible longings. A few days later, she joined them.

That very evening, she told her chief steward, "Tomorrow at dinner I wish to eat little Aurora."

"Surely not, your majesty!" he protested.

"I command it," growled the queen. "And prepare a rich sauce for her."

The poor man knew that one should never play games with an ogre. So, with his knife, he went to little Aurora's bedchamber. The girl was four years old at that time, and she rushed up to him, smiling, and threw her arms around his neck. The steward began to weep, and the knife fell from his hand. Then he dashed into the yard and killed a lamb. He had it cooked in such a wonderful sauce that the queen-mother claimed she had never eaten anything so delicious. In the meantime, he took away little Aurora and his wife hid her in their cottage at the end of the courtyard.

Eight days later, the evil queen-mother announced to the steward, "For supper, I wish to eat Sunshine."

The man decided to deceive the queen-mother as he had before. He found three-year-old Sunshine with

a tiny sword in his hand, fencing with a monkey. The clever man took Sunshine to his wife, who hid him with Aurora. In the boy's place, the steward cooked a young goat. The queen-mother pronounced it delicious.

So far all had gone well, but then one evening the wicked queen-mother said to the chief steward, "I want to eat the queen herself."

The chief steward had no hope of tricking the ogress a third time. To save his own life, he decided that he had no choice but to do as she commanded.

He worked himself up to a rage and went to the young queen's chamber, his mind set. Still, he didn't want to strike her without warning. With great respect, he told her of the queen-mother's command.

"Do your duty," said the young queen bravely. "Carry out the orders that you have received. At least I will now be united with my beloved children!" She believed them dead, for she knew nothing of them since they had been taken from her.

"No, no, your majesty!" cried the steward, his heart softening. "You will not die, and you will see your children again. I have hidden them in my cottage. I will trick the queen-mother once more, and give her a young deer to eat in place of you."

He led the queen to his cottage, where he left her in tears in the arms of her children. Then he cooked a young deer, which the wicked ogress ate greedily. She was quite pleased with her cruelty. She decided to tell her son, upon his return, that savage wolves had devoured his wife and children.

One evening, the queen-mother wandered about the castle courtyards alone. From a distance she heard little Sunshine speaking to his mother. She also heard little Aurora. The ogress recognized the voices of the queen and her children, and she grew furious that she had been tricked.

The next morning, in a voice so frightening that all who heard her trembled, she ordered that a huge tub be placed in the middle of the courtyard. She commanded that it be filled with all sorts of horrid creatures—toads, poisonous vipers, slugs, and

serpents. Her intention was to throw the queen, her two children, the chief steward, his wife, and his serving girl into the tub! When all was ready, she ordered that her victims be brought before her.

There they were, and the executioners were preparing to throw them into the tub. Suddenly, the king, arriving quite unexpectedly, rode into the courtyard. Astonished, he demanded to know the meaning of the horrible spectacle.

The ogress was enraged to see the king arrive. She threw herself into the tub head first, and in an instant, she was devoured by the beasts that she herself had brought together.

Horrified, the king listened to the tale of what had happened in his absence. Then he drew his lovely wife and sweet children to him, and they lived together in love and happiness from that day forward.

The Fairies

Once upon a time, there was a widow who had two daughters. The older girl was so like her mother in looks and behavior that to see one was to see the other. This daughter was ill-tempered and proud, and living with her was impossible. The younger daughter was the image of her father, sweet and honest, the kindest girl that anyone could meet. Yet, because people are always fondest of those who are like themselves, the mother loved her older daughter with all her heart. Her younger daughter she disliked greatly. She made the girl eat in the kitchen and work without stop.

One job the poor girl had was to walk a fair distance to the well twice a day. She had to fill a large jug with water and carry it back. One day, a poor old woman came up to her at the well. "Would you be so kind as to give me a drink from the well?" she asked.

"Certainly, good woman," replied the girl. She lowered her jug into the well and filled it with the purest of water. She even held the jug for the old woman that she might drink more easily. Really, the

old woman was a fairy who had come in disguise to see how far the girl's kindness went.

After she drank, she said, "Child, you are so good, kind, and sweet that I must give you a present. With every word you speak, either a flower or a precious stone will fall from your lips." And as the astonished girl tried to thank her, flowers and jewels cascaded from her mouth.

When the girl returned home, her mother scolded her for being late. "Please forgive me, dear mother, for my lateness," said the girl. As she spoke, red roses, lovely pearls, and sparkling diamonds fell from her lips.

"What is this?" demanded her amazed mother. "Do I see pearls and diamonds flowing from your lips? What is happening, dear daughter?" (This was the first time she called the girl "daughter.")

The girl told what had happened. Without stop, diamonds rained from her mouth. "How wonderful!" exclaimed her mother. "I must send your sister to the well." Then she called to her eldest, "Gertrude, do you see what falls from your sister's mouth as she speaks? Surely you would like to do that. All you have to do is go to the well to fetch water. When a poor old woman asks you for a drink, give her one politely."

"Certainly you don't expect *me* to fetch water from the well!" answered the rude girl.

"Go this instant!" declared her mother.

Gertrude continued to complain, but she went, carrying the best silver jug they had. As soon as she reached the well, a fine lady dressed in magnificent clothes stepped out of the woods and asked for a drink. This was the same fairy who had appeared to Gertrude's sister. Now she came as a princess to see how far Gertrude's kindness went.

"I suppose I've come all this way just to give you something to drink?" the proud girl said to her rudely. "And of course, I have brought a silver jug with me so that *Madam* can have a drink. If you want a drink, get it yourself."

"You are not very kind," said the fairy calmly. "Because of your rudeness, I have a gift for you. For every word you speak, a snake or a toad will spring from your lips." And as Gertrude scoffed, snakes and toads sprang from her lips.

As soon as Gertrude returned home, her mother asked, "Well, my dearest?"

"Well, what, mother dear?" answered the girl, spitting out snakes and toads.

"Oh, no!" exclaimed her mother. "What do I see happening? This is your sister's fault—and she will pay." Then she ran off to find her younger daughter so she could beat her. However, the poor girl fled to the nearby forest.

There, the king's son found her as he was returning home from a hunting trip. He saw how beautiful she was, and that she was sad. "What are you doing all alone in the woods? And why do you weep?" inquired the prince.

"Alas, fine lord, my mother has driven me out of the house." As the words came out of her mouth, so too did roses, five or six pearls, and a number of diamonds.

When the king's son saw this, he begged her to tell him how she had come by such a gift. And so she told him the whole story. As she spoke, the young prince fell in love with her. Knowing that her kindness and the flowers and jewels that it brought were better than any dowry, he took her to his father's palace. There they were wed.

As for the unkind sister, she became so hateful that even her mother drove her from the house. For a long time, the unfortunate girl wandered in the woods, never finding anyone who would take her in. Eventually she died in a dark corner of the forest, alone.

Cinderella

Once upon a time there was a gentleman who took as his second wife the proudest and most arrogant woman ever beheld. She had two daughters of her own who were as much like her in character as two drops of water. The husband had a younger daughter, but she was sweet and kind beyond imagining. In this she took after her own mother, who had been the sweetest and kindest woman in the whole world.

No sooner had the wedding taken place than the stepmother showed her wickedness. She could not bear the good qualities of her husband's young daughter because, by comparison, her own daughters seemed more disagreeable than ever. So she forced the young girl to do the lowliest household chores. It was she who had to scrub the stairs, clean the kitchen, and tidy up the bedrooms of her stepmother and stepsisters. The young girl also had to sleep on a straw mattress beneath the attic roof. Meanwhile the sisters slept in stylish beds in rooms with mirrors in which they could look at themselves from head to foot.

The poor girl endured everything with patience. She dared not complain to her father. He would only have scolded her, since he did everything that his wife asked of him.

When she had finished her household chores, the good girl would go into a corner by the fireplace, and there she would sit on the cinders. This is why she was commonly called Cinderella, meaning "little cinder girl." Yet even in her shabby clothes, Cinderella was a hundred times more beautiful than her stepsisters, who dressed like great ladies.

Now it came to pass that the son of the king was giving a great ball. He invited all the important people in the kingdom. The stepsisters were invited because they were well known in the country. They were

overjoyed, and fluttered about in search of the most ravishing gowns and elaborate coiffures. All this gave more work to Cinderella because it fell to her to iron the sisters' petticoats and to starch their gowns. Throughout the house there was talk of nothing but what the sisters would wear to the ball.

"I," said the older stepsister, "shall wear my red velvet dress with the lace trim."

"I," said the younger, "shall wear my usual dress, but over it I shall drape my gold-flowered cape and diamond necklace."

The sisters sent for the very best hair stylist and had him make two hair bands. From the best shop, they sent off to buy the latest in false beauty marks. Then they called for Cinderella. They had the highest regard for her taste because she always spoke her true mind. Cinderella gave the sisters excellent advice, and she offered to dress them.

While she was dressing them and helping with their hair, the stepsisters asked, "Cinderella, would you like to go to the ball?"

"Ah, my ladies," she said, "you are making fun of me! This is not an amusement for me!"

"How right you are!" the sisters replied. "That would really make us laugh—to see a Cinderella like you at the ball!"

Any other girl, in Cinderella's place, would have deliberately dressed the sisters badly. But she was a good girl, and she helped them to dress well.

For almost two days before the big day, the stepsisters went without eating. Then their dresses could be pulled tight, and their waists would look as thin as a wasp's. They spent all day before the mirror.

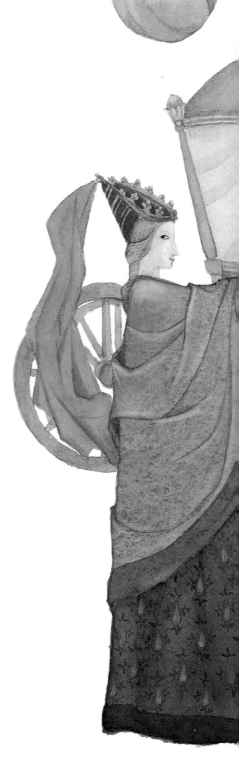

At last the day arrived, and the sisters left the house. Cinderella's gaze followed them until they disappeared from sight. Then she began to cry. Her godmother, coming to her, found her in a sea of tears. She asked what had happened.

"I wish . . . I wish. . . ." Cinderella was crying so hard that she was unable to speak.

The godmother, who was also a fairy, asked, "Would you like to go to the ball, too?"

"Oh, yes, I would," said Cinderella with a sigh.

"Very well. Promise me to be brave, and I shall see that you go," replied the fairy godmother.

She led Cinderella into a room and told her, "Go into the vegetable garden and bring me a pumpkin."

Cinderella ran off to pick the finest pumpkin she could find, and she brought it to the fairy godmother. The fairy godmother scooped out the pumpkin thoroughly. She tapped it with her magic wand, and in a split second the pumpkin turned into a beautiful carriage, made entirely of gold.

Then the fairy godmother went into the pantry to look in the mousetrap. There she found six mice, all still alive. She told Cinderella to open the gate of the mousetrap. As each mouse ran out, she gave it a tap with her magic wand. At that, the mouse turned into a fine horse. In this way, the fairy godmother put together a magnificent team of six horses. Delighted, Cinderella said to her, "Wait a moment. I'll see if the other trap has a fine-looking mouse, so we can make a coachman out of him."

Cinderella returned with the trap, in which there were three large mice. The fairy godmother chose the one with the longest whiskers. No sooner had she touched this mouse than it turned into a fine coachman, with the most splendid whiskers ever seen.

33

Then the fairy godmother told Cinderella, "In the garden, behind the watering can, you will find six lizards. Bring them here."

Cinderella went and brought back the lizards. The fairy godmother changed them instantly into six footmen dressed in livery trimmed with braid. The footmen jumped into place behind the carriage and stood there at attention, as if in all their lives they had never had any other job!

Then the fairy godmother said to Cinderella, "Well, now you have everything you need to go to the ball. Are you happy?"

"Yes," Cinderella answered, "but must I go this way, in the ugly dress that I'm wearing?"

The fairy godmother touched her with the magic wand, and the shabby dress changed into a gown of gold and silver brocade set with jewels. Then she gave Cinderella a pair of marvelous glass dancing shoes. Dressed in splendor, Cinderella climbed into the carriage. But the fairy godmother warned her above all else not to stay at the ball past midnight. If Cinderella were there one minute too long, the carriage would become a pumpkin once again, the horses mere mice, the footmen lizards. Her dress, too, would become as ragged as ever. Cinderella promised to leave the ball before midnight and departed, quite beside herself with happiness.

When the king's son was told that a mysterious princess had arrived at the ball, he hurried forward to receive Cinderella. He helped her from the carriage and led her into the great ballroom. As they entered, a deep silence fell over the room. The dancing broke off. The violins ceased to play. Everyone was gazing upon the beautiful unknown woman. Nothing was heard but a whisper and a murmur of "How lovely she is!"

The king, old as he was, could not help whispering to the queen that he had not seen a woman of such beauty and grace in many years. The ladies could not take their eyes off Cinderella. They studied her hairdo and her gown so that they could try to match them the next day.

The king's son had Cinderella seated in the place of honor. Then he invited her to dance. She danced with such grace that all who beheld her were amazed. Magnificent refreshments were served, but the young prince tasted nothing. He was too busy gazing upon the beautiful woman. After a while, Cinderella went and sat beside her stepsisters. She treated them with

great politeness and offered them the oranges and lemons that the prince had given her. The astonished sisters had not recognized her.

While the three women were talking together, Cinderella heard the clock strike eleven and three-quarters hours. Quickly she made a fine curtsy and left, as swift as the wind.

When she arrived home, Cinderella ran to her fairy godmother and thanked her. She also told the fairy that she would like to go to the ball on the following day, too, because the king's son had begged her to return. While she was still speaking, the two stepsisters returned. Cinderella opened the door.

"How late you are returning!" said Cinderella. She rubbed her eyes and stretched, as if she had awakened that very moment.

"If you had been at the ball," one of the stepsisters said to her, "you would not have been weary. The most beautiful princess the world has ever seen was there. She showed us a thousand courtesies and gave us oranges and lemons."

Cinderella could hardly contain her happiness. She asked the name of the princess, but the sisters replied that they did not know it. They told her, however, that the king's son was dying of longing to discover who the princess was and that he was willing to give a reward to find out. Cinderella smiled and said, "She must truly be beautiful! How fortunate you two are! What I would do to be able to see her!"

The following evening, the two stepsisters returned to the ball. So did Cinderella, even more magnificently dressed than the first time. The king's son did not leave her side, and the whole evening long he showered her with tender and gallant phrases. The maiden, not at all tired, forgot her fairy godmother's

warning. Then suddenly, when she heard the first stroke of midnight, she fled with the lightness of a deer.

The prince ran after Cinderella, but he could not catch up with her. In her flight, she lost one of her little glass shoes, and the prince picked it up most lovingly. Cinderella arrived home out of breath—without the carriage, without footmen, and wearing her ragged, everyday dress. All that remained of her magnificence was one of the glass shoes. The guards of the royal palace were asked if they had by chance seen a princess leave. They reported seeing no one except a girl dressed poorly, more like a peasant than a lady.

When the stepsisters returned from the ball, Cinderella asked them if they had enjoyed themselves and if they had seen the beautiful woman again. They answered yes, adding that the beautiful woman had fled at the stroke of midnight. She had gone with such haste that she had left one of her glass shoes, the prettiest shoe in the world. The king's son had picked it up, they said, and did nothing but gaze admiringly

upon it. That meant that he was madly in love with the beautiful lady to whom the shoe belonged.

And the sister spoke the truth. In fact, a few days later the king's son announced that he would marry the maiden whose foot fit perfectly into the little shoe.

Then began a contest to see whose foot the shoe fit. The duchesses and ladies of the court tried it on, but that was a waste of time. The shoe was carried to the home of the two stepsisters. Each of them made every effort to fit their feet into it, but also without success. Cinderella, who was watching, said "Let's see if it fits on me!"

The stepsisters began to laugh and to make fun of her. But the gentleman who was taking the glass shoe about the kingdom thought that Cinderella seemed very beautiful. He said that it was right for Cinderella to have a turn, for he had been ordered to have all the maidens in the kingdom try the shoe on this day.

He had Cinderella sit down and brought the shoe close to her foot. Immediately, he saw that it fit her

without forcing, as smooth and snug as a hand in a glove.

The sisters' astonishment was great. But it became even greater when Cinderella took from her pocket the other shoe and put it on her other foot.

At this point, the fairy godmother arrived. She gave Cinderella's clothes a touch of her wand, causing them to become even more stunning than before. It was then that the stepsisters recognized Cinderella as the beautiful lady of the ball. They threw themselves at her feet to beg her forgiveness for the ill-treatment they had caused her to suffer. Cinderella made them rise. She embraced them and said that she forgave them with all her heart, and she asked them to wish her well forever. Then, magnificently arrayed, Cinderella was taken to the prince, to whom she seemed more beautiful than ever. After a few days, they were married.

Cinderella was as kindly as she was lovely. She had her two stepsisters come to the palace, and the very same day she gave them in marriage to two gentlemen of the court.

Bluebeard

Once upon a time, there was a man who had beautiful houses in the city and in the country, dishes of gold and silver, fine furniture, and gilded carriages. His misfortune was that he had a blue beard. It made him so frightening that there wasn't a woman or girl who didn't run from the sight of him.

In the area was a noble lady who had two daughters of perfect beauty. The man, called Bluebeard, asked for one of their hands in marriage, whichever girl the mother chose. But neither of the sisters wished to talk with him. They didn't like the idea of having a husband with a blue beard. What made them shudder even more was that he had already had several wives, and no one knew exactly what had happened to them.

To gain the confidence of the young women, Bluebeard escorted them, their mother, and several of their friends to one of his country houses. They were

free to entertain themselves for eight days. The time was spent on long walks in the country, fishing parties, and a round of balls, banquets, and refreshments. There was no time to sleep, because the nights passed in games and gallantry.

Things went so well, in fact, that the younger daughter, Maria, decided that their host didn't have such a blue beard after all. He seemed to her quite a gentleman. And so, as soon as they returned to the city, Maria and Bluebeard married.

After a month, Bluebeard told his wife, "Maria, I find that I must go away on business for six weeks. I do not want you to be sad while I am gone. Invite your friends to stay with you, or go to the country if it pleases you. Above all, be happy."

"Here," he went on, "take my key ring. This is the key to the two large storerooms where I keep the furniture not in use. Here's the key that unlocks the dishes of gold and silver that aren't used every day. And this is the key to my safe, where I keep all of my gold and silver coins. This one is for the jewel case, and here's the master key for all the rooms in the house. This little key opens the little room at the end of the corridor on the ground floor. You may unlock any door and go anywhere you wish except that room. I warn you, if by ill luck you dare to open it, you must expect the worst of my anger!"

Maria promised to obey his command without fail. After they embraced, he got into his carriage and left.

Maria's mother, sister, and friends didn't wait for an invitation to see Bluebeard's stately home. They were all impatient to look at its riches. They hurried about the halls, the bedrooms, and the dressing rooms, each of which was more impressive than the last. They admired the quantity and beauty of the tapestries, sofas, wardrobes, large and small tables, and mirrors in which you could see yourself from head to foot.

Maria's guests couldn't stop praising and envying her good fortune. Maria, however, did not enjoy the sight of all these riches. All she could think of was the little room at the end of the corridor on the ground floor. Finally, leaving her company alone, she rushed into a secret staircase and ran down the steps with breakneck speed. Arriving at the door, she paused briefly, remembering Bluebeard's warning and considering the troubles that her disobedience might bring. But the temptation was too great. With a trembling hand, she unlocked the door with the little key.

At first she saw nothing, for the windows were closed. But after a few minutes, she began to see, along the wall, several long wooden boxes, the size and shape of coffins. Curious about what was in them, she moved closer to see the labels on each. She read one, and another, and then she screamed, "These are the names of Bluebeard's wives!" The key to the room, which she had pulled out of the keyhole, fell from her hand. She had to find it on the floor. Then she locked the door and ran to her room to recover from her fright.

It was then that she noticed that the little key had turned bright red, the color of blood. Maria wiped the key, once, twice, three times, but the color would not

come off. She went to the basin and scrubbed it under water, then scraped it with a pumice stone. Still the red would not come off! The key was bewitched! She yanked it off the key ring and hid it under the bed. She then went down to her guests, told them she wasn't feeling well, and asked all except her sister, Anna, to leave.

When Maria explained to her sister what she had seen, Anna, too, screamed in horror. "I will help you pack your things," she exclaimed. "Hurry!"

But, just then, a door slammed downstairs. "Maria, my dear, I am home," called Bluebeard. The sisters looked at each other with terror in their eyes. Maria went to the door to greet her husband while Anna hid.

"I received a letter," Bluebeard explained, "telling me that my business affairs had been settled without me, and rather well. So I came home early." Maria hugged him, pretending nothing was wrong.

"Now, I would like to have my keys," Bluebeard said. As Maria handed the key ring to him, her hand shook so badly that he guessed immediately what had happened. "Why is the little key to the room on the ground floor missing?" he asked.

Maria replied in an unsteady voice, "Perhaps I left it upstairs on my bedside table."

"Bring it to me at once," Bluebeard demanded.

Maria delayed as long as she could. Soon however, she had no choice but to get the key. She covered the key with her hand as she gave it to him, hoping that he would not look at it.

He examined the key and said to his wife, "Why is this key the color of blood?"

"I don't know," said the poor woman, whiter than death.

"Ah, you don't know!" answered Bluebeard. "But I do! You wanted to go into the little room! Well, lady, now you will take your place with the others!"

"Please, please, forgive me," cried Maria. "I did not mean to open the door. I couldn't help myself." She flung herself at his feet. "I will never go in there again. Please, husband . . ."

But Bluebeard's heart was harder than stone. "You must die," he said, "and at once!"

"If I must die," Maria sobbed, "please give me some time to make my peace with God."

"I will grant you fifteen minutes, but not a second longer." And Bluebeard left the room.

As soon as she was alone, the poor woman called to her sister, "Anna, oh Anna, run to the top of the tower and watch for our brothers. They were to return from the country today. If you see them, wave to them to come quickly. Go!"

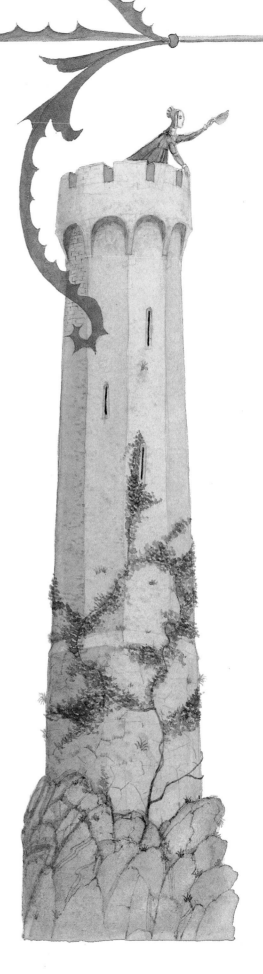

Anna went up to the tower. Minutes later, Maria called, "Anna, Anna, don't you see anyone coming?"

"I can only see the sun shining on the waving grass," Anna answered.

Meanwhile, Bluebeard, with a knife in his hand, cried out at the top of his voice, "Come down at once, or I am coming up."

"Just one more minute," implored Maria. She again called softly, "Anna, can you see anyone?"

Her sister Anna replied, "I can see only the sun shining on the waving grass."

"Come down at once!" yelled Bluebeard. "Or I come up!"

"I am coming," Maria answered. And again she

called up to her sister, "Anna, Anna, can't you see anyone coming?"

"I see," answered Anna, "a large cloud of dust drawing near!"

"Is it our brothers?" cried Maria.

"Alas, no, my sister, it's a herd of sheep!"

"Are you coming down, yes or no?" cried Bluebeard.

"Just a minute more," answered Maria. Again she called, "Anna, Anna, can you see anyone coming?"

"I see," answered Anna, "two horsemen, but they are still far off." Just a minute later, she exclaimed, "It *is* our brothers! I'm signalling them to come fast."

But Bluebeard began shouting so loudly that the whole house shook. Maria had no choice but to come down lest she give away her sister, her only hope. She threw herself at Bluebeard's feet, weeping.

"It is useless to weep," said her husband. "You must die!" Grabbing her with one hand, he raised his knife with the other. But, at that very moment, there came such a loud knocking that he froze. The door burst open, and Maria's two brothers charged in. They drew their swords and threw themselves on Bluebeard. To save himself, Bluebeard had to flee, but the brothers chased and caught him before he reached the door of the house. There was a short fight, and then Bluebeard was dead. The poor woman was almost as dead as her husband, and had not the strength to rise and embrace her brothers.

Afterwards, it was discovered that Bluebeard had no family. Therefore, Maria became the owner of all his possessions. She gave generous portions to her sister and her brothers. Later, Maria married a fine gentleman, who made her forget all the heartbreak she had suffered with Bluebeard.

Hop O' My Thumb

Once upon a time, there lived a woodcutter, his wife, and their seven sons. The oldest was ten years old, and the youngest seven. Is it surprising that the children could be this close in age? The fact is that they were three sets of twins and another child, the youngest. The woodcutter and his wife were very poor, and the seven sons were a great burden, for they were too young to earn a living.

Their greatest worry, however, was that the littlest, other than being frail, spoke very seldom. He was very small and, when he came into this world, seemed no larger than a thumb. For this reason he was called Hop O' My Thumb. The poor little boy was often teased and talked about, but he was more intelligent than any of his brothers. Although he did not often talk, he listened a lot.

There came a difficult year, and the woodcutter could not buy food for his family. The poor father became so hopeless that he decided the sons could no longer live with them. One evening, when the boys were in bed, he and his wife sat by the fire talking.

The woodcutter said, "I see that we can no longer feed our sons. But I can't watch them die of starvation before our eyes. I think that we should go to the woods tomorrow and leave them there. It won't be difficult. While the boys are busy gathering wood, we will run away without them noticing."

"Alas!" his wife exclaimed. "How can we abandon our sons?"

The woodcutter reminded her of their great poverty, but the woman still argued. She was poor but she was, nevertheless, the boys' mother. Her husband persisted, "It would be more painful to watch them suffer and die in our own home, would it not?"

His wife could only nod her head and cry.

Hop O' My Thumb had heard everything because, recognizing that they were talking about important matters, he had sneaked out of bed and hid beneath his father's chair. Now he crept back up to bed. He spent the rest of the night thinking of what to do.

Early the next morning, Hop O' My Thumb got up and went down to the stream. He filled a little sack with white pebbles and returned home.

Soon the family set out, and Hop O' My Thumb revealed nothing of what he knew to his brothers. They walked into a very dense forest, where at a distance they couldn't see one another.

The woodcutter began to chop wood, and his seven sons began gathering branches into bundles. While the boys' attention was on their task, the woodcutter and his wife slipped away along a little-used path.

When the boys discovered that they were alone, they began to cry and call out at the tops of their voices. Hop O' My Thumb let them do so, even though he knew that they could get back home. At last he said to his brothers, "Do not be afraid. Papa and Mama have left, but I can guide us back home safely. I have left a trail of pebbles along the way. You just have to follow me."

So his brothers followed Hop O' My Thumb and he led them home. When they reached the cottage, they didn't dare enter, but crept close to the door to hear what their parents were saying.

"Oh dear, where do you think our poor children are now?" lamented their mother. "Who would have thought our fortune would change the very same day

57

that we sent them away? Now that the lord of the manor has paid us the ten silver pieces he owed us, we have more than enough to eat. If only our children could have eaten as fine a meal as we just had! What can they be doing in the forest now? Suppose the wolves are eating them! Oh, why did we leave them? I knew we'd be sorry. Where are my poor boys now?"

At that, the boys banged on the door and shouted, "We're here! We're all here!" The woodcutter's wife threw open the door. The boys scrambled inside, hugged their parents, and cried with joy.

"How happy we are that you've come back!" their mother exclaimed.

The boys sat down at the table and ate with an appetite that pleased their father and mother. As they ate, they chattered away, telling of their time in the forest and the pebble trail that Hop O' My Thumb had made.

The parents were overjoyed to have their boys back home again, but the joy lasted only as long as the ten silver coins. When the money was spent, they were plunged back into misery. And once more, they decided to abandon their children. This time, they agreed, they would take the boys farther away.

They couldn't avoid being overheard by Hop O'
My Thumb. He counted on doing what he had done
before. But when he got up early the next morning to
go out for pebbles, he couldn't get out. The door was
locked. However, when his mother gave each child a
slice of bread for breakfast, Hop O' My Thumb
thought of spreading breadcrumbs instead of pebbles
and he slipped the bread into his pocket.

After breakfast, the woodcutter and his wife took
the boys to the thickest part of the forest. As soon as
the children were at work, the woodcutter and his
wife ran away, leaving them behind. The boys cried
and called out again. And again, Hop O' My Thumb
stopped them, saying, "You need not worry. I have
left a path of breadcrumbs. We will follow it and be
safe at home in no time." But as he tried to lead his
brothers out of the woods, he looked ahead for his
trail and saw that birds had eaten every crumb.

Now the boys felt truly without hope. The farther
they walked, the more lost they became, plunging
deeper and deeper into the forest. Darkness fell, and a

60

strong wind came up, frightening them even more. All around, it seemed, they heard the howling of wolves coming to eat them. No one dared to say a word or even turn around to look! Then a heavy shower fell and soaked them all to the bone. When it was over, the children slipped and fell in the mud with every step, getting dirty and scratched as they went.

Hop O' My Thumb climbed up to the top of a tall tree to look around. He caught sight of a small

light no brighter than a candle and far away, beyond the forest. He came down from the tree, but he could not see the light from the ground. He almost despaired again. Nevertheless, after walking a bit with his brothers in the direction of the light, Hop O' My Thumb went up another tree and saw the light again. He had to climb many trees during the night to keep on track. Exhausted, the group finally came upon the house with the candle burning in the window.

They knocked on the door, and a woman opened it and asked what they wanted.

"My brothers and I are lost." said Hop O' My Thumb. "We have lost our way. We are hungry and tired. Do you think you could find it in your heart to shelter us for the night?"

The woman, seeing how young they were, began to cry and said, "Oh, dear, poor children! You should never have come here! Don't you know that this is the house of an ogre who eats fine, young children such as you?"

"What can we do now?" cried Hop O' My Thumb, trembling like his brothers. "The wolves will eat us in the forest tonight if you don't give us shelter. We'd be better off risking the ogre's stomach! Perhaps he will take pity on us if only you will ask him to."

The ogre's wife agreed to hide them from her husband. "Please come in and warm yourselves by the fire," she said. Over the fire, a whole sheep was roasting for the ogre's supper.

As the boys sat warming themselves, they heard three or four great knocks at the door. The ogre had come home! Quickly, the wife hid the boys under the bed before she opened the door and her husband, the ogre, thundered in. Immediately, he sat down at the table and consumed the entire sheep, which was cooked rare, just as he liked it. Next he began to sniff the air.

"I smell fresh meat," he roared.

"It must be the calf I've been preparing for breakfast," said his wife.

"No, it's fresh meat I smell," insisted the ogre. "There's something strange going on in my house," the ogre continued, looking around as he spoke. And

the ogre went straight over to the bed and peered beneath it.

"Ah, so this is how you deceive me!" he cried. He pulled the children out from under the bed one at a time. They all fell to their knees, begging for mercy, but they were in the hands of the most hard-hearted ogre in the world. Far from feeling pity, he said, "I'm beginning to feel hungry again just looking at you." He took his knife and sharpened it on a stone.

But when he went to grab one of the boys, his wife said, "You just had your supper! Why not have the boys tomorrow?"

"Why should I wait?" asked the ogre.

"We happen to have lots of meat in the house at present. There's a calf, two sheep, and a half a pig," his wife replied.

"Maybe you are right," said the ogre grudgingly.

"But see that you give them plenty to eat to fatten them up. Then put them to bed."

The ogre's wife sighed with relief as she brought the hungry boys a fine dinner. But they were so frightened they could barely eat, so she took them up to bed.

Now it happened that the ogre had seven daughters. They were little ogres who showed every sign of growing up in their father's tradition, because they ate fresh meat as ogres do. Each one had little gray eyes, a bent nose, and an enormous mouth with long, sharp teeth! They were not yet very wicked, but no doubt they would be in time. The daughters had gone to bed early, and all seven lay in one great big bed, each with a crown on her head. In the same room

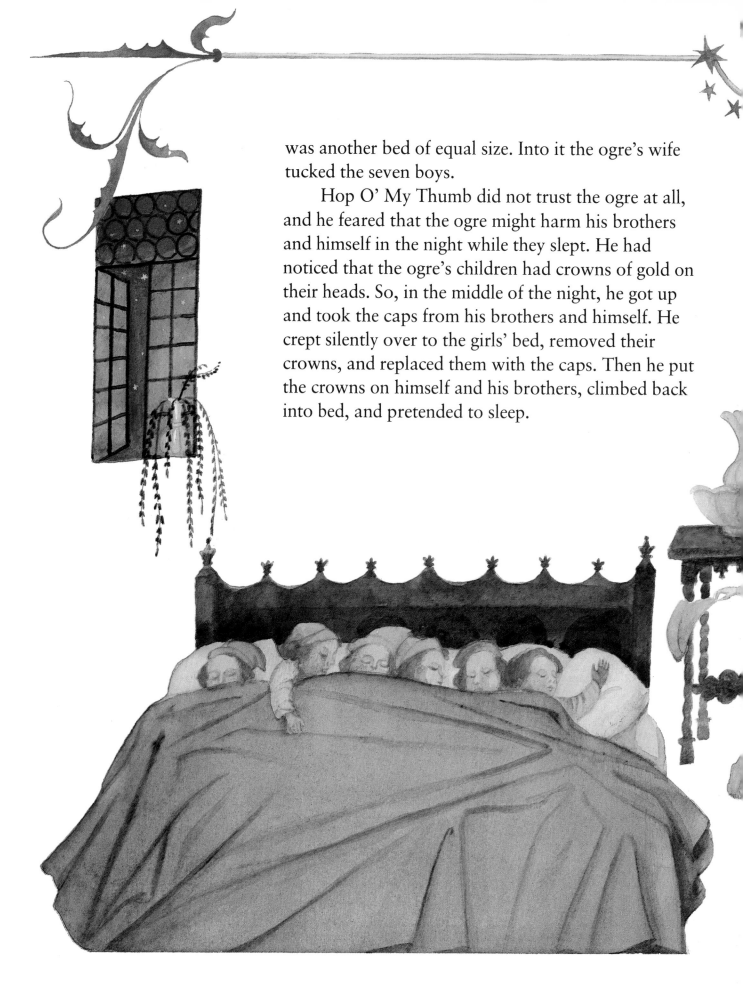

was another bed of equal size. Into it the ogre's wife tucked the seven boys.

Hop O' My Thumb did not trust the ogre at all, and he feared that the ogre might harm his brothers and himself in the night while they slept. He had noticed that the ogre's children had crowns of gold on their heads. So, in the middle of the night, he got up and took the caps from his brothers and himself. He crept silently over to the girls' bed, removed their crowns, and replaced them with the caps. Then he put the crowns on himself and his brothers, climbed back into bed, and pretended to sleep.

Just as Hop O' My Thumb suspected, into the bedroom crept the ogre, not wanting to leave till tomorrow what he could do the same night. He tiptoed over to the boys' bed. "Ah, I must have gotten confused in my excitement," the ogre said as he reached for the first boy. "I can feel crowns on these heads. These must be my daughters." So saying, he went over to the other bed. "Yes, here are the boys. I can tell them by their caps. It's a good thing I've got my wits about me," said the ogre, and he slew them in a flash.

Then, with a sigh of satisfaction, the ogre went back to bed.

As soon as Hop O' My Thumb heard the ogre's rumbling snores, he jumped out of bed and began shaking his brothers from their sleep. "Get dressed and follow me," he whispered. The brothers did as Hop O' My Thumb asked. When they were ready, they tiptoed out of the house and climbed over the garden wall. They ran off into the night, though they could hardly see the path.

In the morning when he awoke, the ogre said to his wife, "Go upstairs and bring those plump little fellows down here." His wife, thinking that he wanted her to get them dressed and give them a hearty breakfast, was amazed at her husband's kindness. She went upstairs to wake the boys and her daughters.

When she entered the room, she screamed in horror at what she found. When the ogre rushed upstairs to see what the fuss was about, he became enraged.

"What have I done?" he roared. "I have been tricked! This is all their fault. They will pay dearly for this!" He ran to the cupboard and took out his seven-league boots. In these boots, he could travel seven leagues in a single step. The ogre put them on and marched out of the house.

The boys were back in the woods, nearing their home, when they looked back. To their dismay, there was the ogre leaping from mountain to mountain and crossing rivers as if they were trickles of water. Hop O' My Thumb saw a cave in a rock not far from himself and his brothers, and he had the group hide there, where they could see what the ogre was doing.

The ogre arrived at the spot instantly, but he was thoroughly exhausted because seven-league boots are most difficult to wear. Too tired to move, he lay down

for a rest on the top of the rock in which the boys were hidden. He was fast asleep in no time and snoring thunderously. The poor boys felt the same terror as when he had first pulled them from under the bed and threatened to kill them.

Hop O' My Thumb was less frightened than the others. He told his brothers to escape and run home, and not to worry about him. As usual, his brothers followed Hop O' My Thumb's orders without question.

As soon as his brothers were out of danger, Hop O' My Thumb crept over to the ogre. He gently pulled the seven-league boots off the sleeping giant's feet. Then he pulled the boots over his own feet. Because they were magic boots, they instantly shrank to fit his feet perfectly. Once the boots were his, he bounded off, back to the ogre's house. When he arrived, he found the ogre's wife still crying over her daughters.

Hop O' My Thumb said to her, "Your husband is in great danger. He has been captured by a band of

thieves even more frightening than the ogre himself!
They say they will kill him if he does not give them all
his gold and silver. While they were holding him, he
saw me and begged me to tell you what has happened.
He beseeches you to give me all your valuables, or
they will kill him. Because of the urgency of the
situation, he has lent me his seven-league boots, as you
can see, so that I could get here and back more
quickly. Also, he knew that the boots would prove I'm
not an imposter."

The ogre's wife was terrified and believed it wise
to follow her husband's directive. Without hesitating
even for a moment, she gave Hop O' My Thumb all of
their riches, which he took home and gave to his
family.

Now many people say that is not the way the
story really ended. They say that Hop O' My Thumb
took only the ogre's boots, just to make sure that he
could never chase after any more children. They claim
to know the facts of what he did after that because
they ate and drank at the woodcutter's home.

According to these reports, once he had the
boots, Hop O' My Thumb went straight to the king's
royal court to see if he could be of some service. The
king asked Hop O' My Thumb to bring news of the
army, which was fighting far, far away, and of the
results of a battle that was raging. Hop O' My Thumb
promised to bring him word that very evening, if he
wanted it. The king offered a great amount of money
as a reward for success. Thanks to the seven-league
boots, Hop O' My Thumb brought back the news on
time, and the king rewarded him very well for his
cleverness.

After that, lords and ladies of the court paid him for carrying messages from one place to another very quickly. (He was paid the best for carrying love letters.) Hop O' My Thumb soon became enormously wealthy. He returned to his family and shared his fortune with them.

Whichever way the story really ended, it is needless to say that Hop O' My Thumb's family greeted him with great joy. They all lived in fine style and were never hungry again.

Puss in Boots

There once was an old miller who, when he died, left his mill, his donkey, and his cat to his three sons. The sons easily divided these things among themselves. The eldest son received the mill, the second got the donkey, and the youngest was left with the cat. The poor lad was most upset at receiving such a poor inheritance. He said to himself, "If my two brothers work together, they can make an honest living. As for me, what good is a cat? I'll soon die of hunger!"

The cat heard all this but pretended not to. He said with a serious manner, "Do not fear, master. Just give me a sack and a pair of hunting boots, and I'll show you that you haven't done so badly!"

Although the cat's new owner was not convinced, he remembered seeing the animal using some clever tricks to catch rats and mice. For instance, he hung from the rafters by his feet, or hid in the flour, pretending to be dead. So the lad thought that maybe

77

the cat could help him out of his misery. When the cat had what he had asked for, he put on the boots and flung the sack over his shoulder. Then he set off toward an area where there were large numbers of rabbits. The cat put some ears of wheat and some lettuce leaves into the sack. After that, he lay down and pretended to be dead. He was waiting for some poor rabbit, unused to the wicked ways of the world, to hop into the bag for the food that was inside.

In no time, the cat had his first success. An inexperienced little rabbit hopped into the sack and the cunning cat immediately pulled the string, trapping the rabbit. Pleased with his hunting skills, the cat went straight to the palace and asked to speak to the king. He was taken into the royal apartment. There, with a deep bow, the cat said, "Sire, I bring you a wild rabbit. My lord, the Marquis of Carabas (a made-up name—the first one that came to the cat's mind) commanded me to bring it to you as a gift."

"Tell your master," the king replied, "that I thank him and appreciate his kindness."

Another time, the cat hid in the wheat field, taking his sack with him again. When two partridges entered, he pulled the string and caught them both. Then he took them to the king just as he had done with the rabbit. The king happily accepted the two partridges and offered the cat some milk in return.

The cat continued to bring to the king gifts of game from his master, the Marquis of Carabas. One day, the cat learned that the king planned to go for a ride along the riverbank with his daughter, the most beautiful princess imaginable. He told his master, "If you follow my advice, your fortune will soon be made. Just take a bath in the river at a place I will show you. Then leave the rest to me."

"The Marquis of Carabas" did what his cat advised him, though he had no idea what good it would do him. While the marquis was bathing, the king passed by. The cat began to shout at the top of his voice, "Help, help, the Marquis of Carabas is drowning!"

Hearing these cries, the king put his head out of his carriage window. He recognized the cat who had brought him so many gifts of game and ordered his guards to go to the aid of the Marquis of Carabas. As they were dragging the poor marquis from the river, the cat approached the carriage. He told the king that while his master had been in the water, thieves had come and stolen away his clothes. (The cat had actually hidden them beneath a big rock.)

The king immediately sent one of his officers back to the palace to fetch some of his finest clothes for the Marquis of Carabas.

The king treated the young man very kindly. And, because he looked so good in the fine clothes—for he was a handsome, well-built young man—the king's daughter liked him as well. After just two or three respectful but tender glances from the Marquis of Carabas, the princess fell hopelessly in love with him! The king insisted that the young man join them in their carriage and enjoy the outing with them.

Seeing that his plan was working, the cat ran on ahead. He came across some peasants cutting hay in a field. He said to them, "Good people, you must tell the king that these fields belong to the Marquis of Carabas. If you don't, you will be cut to pieces like sliced ham!" Soon the king passed by and asked them whose fields they were working. The cat's threat had frightened them, so they replied together, "They belong to the Marquis of Carabas."

"You have some fine land," the king said to the Marquis of Carabas.

"As you can see," replied the marquis, "these fields provide a good crop each year."

The cunning cat ran on farther ahead and met with some workers stacking freshly cut wheat. "Good harvesters," he said, "you must tell the king that all this wheat belongs to the Marquis of Carabas. If you don't, you will be chopped into mincemeat!"

The king, who passed a minute later, asked to whom the crops belonged. The peasants replied, "The Marquis of Carabas." The king commended the marquis on his fertile land.

The cat continued to run ahead of the carriage, saying the same thing to everybody he met. The king was amazed at the vast possessions of the Marquis of Carabas.

The cat finally came to a beautiful castle that belonged to the richest ogre there ever was. All the land the king had passed through belonged to the ogre's castle. The cat had taken care to find out who this ogre was and to know what he did. Now he asked to speak with the ogre, saying that it would be rude to pass by his castle without dropping in to pay his respects. The ogre received him with as much kindness as might be expected from an ogre.

"I have been told," said the cat, "that you have the ability to change into any kind of animal—even a lion or an elephant."

"It's true," replied the ogre harshly. "And to prove it, I will change into a lion."

The cat was so frightened to find himself face to face with a lion that he scuttled up onto the roof. This gave him some difficulty, for his tall boots were not suitable for going out onto roof tiles.

After a bit, when the ogre had changed back into his usual shape, the cat came back down. He admitted being very afraid. "I have also been assured," he went on, "that you can also change yourself into a very small animal, like a mouse or a rat. I must confess I find that impossible to believe."

"Impossible?" bellowed the ogre. "Watch this!" He immediately changed into a mouse that began running about on the floor. As soon as the cat saw this, he leaped upon him and gobbled him up!

Meanwhile the king saw, in passing, the castle of the ogre, and he wanted to go inside. Hearing the sound of the carriage on the drawbridge, the cat rushed out and said, "Your majesty, welcome to the castle of the Marquis of Carabas."

"Why, sir!" exclaimed the king. "This castle is yours as well? I have never seen anything as beautiful as this courtyard, with these buildings around it. May we go inside?"

The marquis gave his arm to the young princess and they followed the king into a huge hall. There they found a banquet laid out. The ogre had prepared it for some friends he had been expecting that day. The friends, however, didn't dare enter when they

learned the king was there. The king was as enchanted by the excellent qualities of the Marquis of Carabas as was his daughter, who was obviously head over heels in love.

After considering the vast wealth the marquis seemed to possess, the king turned to the young man and said, "Well, sir, it is up to you if you wish to become my son-in-law!"

Bowing deeply, the marquis accepted the honor, and he and the princess were wedded that very day. The cat became a great lord and never again ran after mice—except for fun.

Ricky-of-the-Tuft

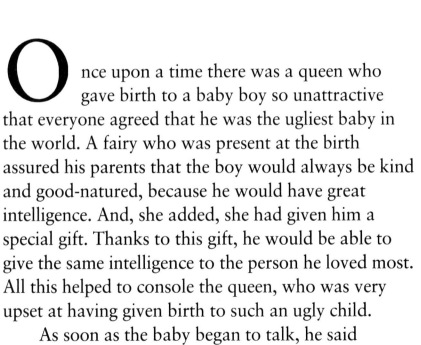

Once upon a time there was a queen who gave birth to a baby boy so unattractive that everyone agreed that he was the ugliest baby in the world. A fairy who was present at the birth assured his parents that the boy would always be kind and good-natured, because he would have great intelligence. And, she added, she had given him a special gift. Thanks to this gift, he would be able to give the same intelligence to the person he loved most. All this helped to console the queen, who was very upset at having given birth to such an ugly child.

As soon as the baby began to talk, he said remarkably sweet things. There was something so clever about everything he did that everyone was charmed by him. I forgot to say that the boy was born with a little tuft of hair on his head. The boy's parents had named him Ricky, but everyone called him Ricky-of-the-Tuft.

A few years later, the queen of a neighboring country gave birth to twin girls. The first-born twin was more beautiful than the sun. This made the queen so happy that she was almost dizzy from excitement. The same fairy who had been present at the birth of Ricky-of-the-Tuft witnessed this birth as well. To temper the queen's delight at having such a beautiful daughter, she warned her that this princess would not be very intelligent. In fact, the princess would be as stupid as she was beautiful. Although this shocked the queen, she was even more dismayed when she saw that her second twin was extremely ugly.

"Do not despair, your majesty," said the fairy. "This daughter will make up for her appearance in other ways. She will be so intelligent that hardly anyone will notice her lack of beauty."

"I certainly hope so!" replied the queen. "But is there no way to get some intelligence for my first-born twin, who is so beautiful?"

"I can do nothing to help her, your majesty, as far as intelligence is concerned," said the fairy, "but I can do anything for her concerning beauty. Since I would very much like to grant your wish, I will give her the ability to make the person whom she loves best as beautiful as herself."

As the twin princesses grew, the whole kingdom spoke of the beauty of the first-born twin and the noble spirit of the second. But as they grew, so too did their drawbacks. The second-born twin became more and more ugly and the first twin became more stupid and clumsy. Either she didn't answer when spoken to or she talked nonsense. She couldn't set out four pieces of china without breaking one, or take a drink of water without spilling some on her clothes.

Although the pretty girl caught people's eyes first, they soon discovered that they preferred the company of the more intelligent twin. It was strange how, within fifteen minutes, the beautiful twin would find herself all alone. Even though she was stupid, she was aware of this. She would gladly have given all of her beauty for less than half of her sister's intelligence.

The queen, smart as she was, couldn't help scolding the first-born twin for her stupidity, and this caused the poor princess even more pain.

One day the beautiful princess was alone in the woods, crying over her misfortunes when an ugly little man dressed in fine clothes approached her. It was the young prince, Ricky-of-the-Tuft. He had fallen in love with her from the many portraits that he had seen of her. He had left his father's kingdom determined to meet this beauty and speak with her.

Happy to find her all alone, Ricky introduced himself with as much respect and good manners as possible. As he did so, he realized that she was unhappy. He said, "I don't see how someone as beautiful as you can seem so sad. I must say, I have seen many beautiful people, but never have I met anyone more lovely or fair than you."

"You are very kind to say that, sir," the princess replied. Ricky-of- the-Tuft went on, "Beauty is such a great privilege that it outdoes all others. When a person possesses beauty, I can't see how anything could cause sadness."

The princess replied, "I would rather be as ugly as you and have some intelligence, than have my beauty and be as stupid as I am."

"Your highness, nothing shows better that people have intelligence than if they believe that they do not have it. It is the nature of the gift that, the more humans have, the more they are certain they don't have any."

"I don't know if that is true," said the princess. "But I do know that I am stupid, and the sadness that causes is killing me."

"If that is all that is worrying you, your highness, I can soon put an end to your suffering."

"How can you do that?" asked the princess.

"I have the power," began Ricky-of-the-Tuft, "to

bestow great intelligence on the person I love the most. Since you, my princess, are that person, it is up to you to accept the gift. All you have to do is agree to marry me."

The princess could not believe her ears and said nothing. Ricky-of-the-Tuft continued. "I see that this proposal makes you uncomfortable, and I am not surprised. I will grant you a whole year to decide."

Because the princess had so little intelligence, and at the same time wanted it so much, she fooled herself into thinking that the end of the year would never come. So she accepted Ricky's proposal right away.

As soon as she had promised to marry Ricky-of-the-Tuft, the princess immediately began to feel different. Suddenly she found it unbelievably easy to say whatever she wanted to in an elegant yet natural way. She had a witty, clever conversation with Ricky-of-the-Tuft. In fact, she demonstrated such brilliance that he began to wonder if he had given her more wit than he had kept for himself!

When the princess returned to the palace, the whole court was amazed at such a sudden, extraordinary change. All the stupid things that she might have said before were replaced by sensible remarks. The whole court was filled with joy. Only her twin was not happy. Without the advantage of greater intelligence, she became completely overshadowed by her sister.

The king now allowed himself to be guided by the beautiful princess's opinions. Sometimes he even held council meetings in her chambers. When word of this change in the beautiful princess spread, all the young princes from the neighboring kingdoms did their best to win her favor. Almost all of them asked for her hand in marriage. But she did not find any of them intelligent enough for her. She listened to all without pledging herself to any.

At last, one came along who was so rich, so handsome, and so intelligent, that the princess could not avoid feeling attracted to him. When her father noticed this, he told her that she was completely free to choose her own husband.

In situations like this, the more intelligent people are, the more difficult it is for them to make a firm decision. So the princess thanked her father and asked him for some time to think it over. She went off by

92

herself to consider her choices, and found, by chance, that she was in the same woods where she had met Ricky-of-the-Tuft.

As the princess was walking along, deep in thought, she heard a rumble beneath her feet. It sounded like many people coming and going. Listening more intently, she heard a voice saying, "Pass me that pot." Another said, "Give me that kettle." Yet another called, "Put some wood on the fire."

Then the ground opened up before her and she saw a huge kitchen full of cooks and waiters and servants. They were all preparing a magnificent banquet. A team of twenty or thirty of them came out and set up a long table in a clearing in the woods. Then all together, with their utensils in their hands, they began working busily to the rhythms of a merry tune. The princess was amazed at this sight. She asked for whom they were working.

"My lady," replied the leader of the company, "we work for Prince Ricky-of-the-Tuft. He is getting married tomorrow."

The princess was even more amazed when she heard this. All of a sudden she remembered that just a

95

year ago, nearly to the day, she had promised to marry Prince Ricky-of-the-Tuft. She suddenly grew faint. There were good reasons for her not remembering her promise. A year ago she had been stupid, and when the prince had given her intelligence, she had completely forgotten all her past stupidity. The princess began to walk on, but she had taken only a few steps when she found herself face to face with Ricky-of-the-Tuft. He was all dressed up and very excited, as befitting a prince who was just about to be married.

"Here I am, your highness," he called. "I have come to keep my word, and no doubt you are here to keep your promise as well. You will make me the happiest of men by granting me your hand in marriage."

"I must confess honestly," replied the princess, "that I have not yet made up my mind. I fear I will never make the decision that you are hoping for."

"I am shocked!" exclaimed Ricky-of-the-Tuft.

"No doubt you are," responded the princess, "and if I were dealing with an insensitive man of lowly birth, I would be very embarrassed. A princess must keep her word, he would say, so I must marry, because I promised to do so. However, since I am speaking to the most understanding man in the world, I am sure that you will see my predicament. You know that even when I was stupid, I was unable to make up my mind about getting married. How do you expect me to be able to reach a decision like this now? After all, with all the intelligence that you have given me, I am even more particular about people. You made a mistake in taking away my stupidity and letting me see things more clearly."

Ricky-of-the-Tuft replied, "If, as you say, you would accept disapproval from a stupid man for not keeping your word, how do you expect me not to be upset with you? Keep in mind that we are discussing the happiness of the rest of my life. Is it right to put intelligent people at a disadvantage compared to

stupid ones? But let us return to the facts. Apart from my homeliness, is there something, perhaps, that you do not like about me? Are you uncomfortable with my background, intelligence, character, or manners?"

"Not at all," replied the princess. "In fact, those are the very things that I am attracted by in you."

"If that is the case," continued Ricky-of-the-Tuft, "then I am very happy, because you have the power to turn me into the most handsome of men!"

"But how could that be possible?" the princess asked him.

"It will happen," he answered, "if you love me enough to want it to happen. Let me remove any doubt from your mind, your highness. That same fairy who gave me the gift of sharing my intelligence with the one I love, also gave you the gift of making the man that you love handsome, if you so wish it."

"If that is so," said the princess, "then I wish with all my heart that you will become the most handsome prince in the world."

No sooner had the princess spoken these words, than Ricky-of-the-Tuft appeared before her eyes as the most handsome, graceful, and fascinating man in the whole world.

Some people said afterwards that it was not the fairy's spell that brought about this change, but love itself. They said that the princess considered carefully her lover's persistence and all the other wonderful qualities in his character and spirit. With these charms in her mind, the princess no longer noticed the imperfections of his body or the ugliness of his features. His stoop seemed but the charming habit of a man shrugging his shoulders. And the limp in his walk became a mannerism that she found endearing. She

saw only love in his bright crossed eyes, and decided that what she had first considered to be a hooked nose was instead heroic.

In any event, the princess promised to marry Ricky as soon as her father, the king, gave his permission. Knowing that his daughter was in love with Ricky-of-the-Tuft, and that the prince had deep understanding and great wisdom, the king was happy to welcome him into the family.

The wedding was celebrated the next day, just as Ricky-of-the-Tuft had foreseen, and people came from far and wide to enjoy the magnificent feast.

Classic Fairy Tales

BY HANS CHRISTIAN ANDERSEN

ILLUSTRATED BY MICHAEL FIODOROV

VOLUME TWO

Table of Contents

Thumbelina   5

The Tinderbox   29

The Steadfast Tin Soldier   45

The Emperor's New Clothes   53

The Swineherd   65

The Nightingale of the Emperor   77

The Princess and the Pea   98

Publisher's Note

The stories of Danish author Hans Christian Andersen (1805–1875) have been delighting children and adults for over 150 years. Of his early stories, Andersen once noted that he wrote them exactly as he would have told them to a child—a telling comment, given the spirited, conversational style of most of the author's tales. We can hear that storyteller's voice relating the adventures of tiny Thumbelina, the brave little tin soldier, the pompous emperor with his glorious but invisible wardrobe, and other memorable characters. "Oh, my gosh!" "Oh, no!" "Now this was a proper husband!" Exclamations abound in Andersen!

Andersen based a few of his tales, namely early ones that include "The Swineherd" and "The Tinderbox," on old Danish folk tales he had known as a child. For the most part, however, Andersen created his own stories—156 in total—and he is not primarily known as a collector of folk tales. Seven of Andersen's most well-known stories are included in this volume, illustrated with classic, delicate beauty by artist Michael Fiodorov.

Thumbelina

O nce upon a time there was a woman who wanted more than anything to have a tiny little child. She had no idea where to get one, so she went to an old witch and told her, "I want so much to have a tiny little child. Could you please tell me where I could get one?"

"That's easy," replied the witch. "Take this grain of barleycorn. It is not the kind that grows in the fields or that the chickens eat. Put it in a flowerpot and then see what happens."

"Thank you!" said the woman, and she gave the witch twelve pennies. Then she went straight home and planted the barleycorn. A lovely great flower sprang up right away. It looked exactly like a tulip, except the petals were tightly closed in a bud.

"What a beautiful flower!" said the woman, and she kissed the red and yellow petals. As soon as she kissed it, the flower opened with a *pop!* She could see now that it was a real tulip, but right in the center, sat a tiny little girl. She was lovely and delicate and no

bigger than your thumb, so the woman decided to name the little girl Thumbelina.

A polished walnut shell became Thumbelina's cradle. Violet petals were her mattress, and a rose petal was her cover. In the daytime, she played on the table. The woman had placed a bowl of water there, with a wreath of flowers around it. Thumbelina sat on a large tulip petal that floated on the water, and she could row from one side of the bowl to the other, using two white horsehairs as oars. It was such a pretty sight! She could sing, too, and she had the sweetest voice you ever heard.

One night, as Thumbelina lay sleeping in her pretty little bed, an old toad hopped into the house through a broken windowpane. The toad was a big, wet, ugly thing, and she jumped right down on the table where Thumbelina was sleeping under her rose petal.

"She would make a lovely wife for my son!" said the toad, and then she grabbed the walnut shell and hopped back into the garden.

A broad stream flowed through the bottom of the garden. It had a muddy bank, and here the toad lived with her son. He was every bit as ugly and horrible as his mother.

"Croak, croak, ribit!" was all he could say when he saw pretty little Thumbelina in her walnut shell bed.

"Don't talk so loud, or you'll wake her!" said the old toad. "She could still run away. And we wouldn't be able to catch her, for she is as light as a swan's down. I will put her on one of the lily pads in the middle of the stream. She is so small it will be like an island for her and she won't be able to escape. In the meantime, we will prepare a fine room in the mud, where you will live together when you are married."

Growing in the stream were lots of water lilies with broad green leaves that floated on the surface. The biggest leaf was the farthest away, and that's where the old toad left the walnut shell. Thumbelina was still sleeping inside.

When the poor little girl woke up in the morning, she saw where she was and began to cry bitterly. The big green lily pad had water all around it, and she couldn't possibly reach the bank.

The old toad stayed busy down in the mud, decorating a room with rushes and yellow water lilies. She wanted to make it pretty for her new daughter-in-law. When she finished, she and her ugly son swam back to the lily pad where they had left Thumbelina. They wanted to fetch her bed and bring it to the bridal chamber.

The old toad curtsied to Thumbelina and said, "This is my son. He's to be your husband. The two of you will live together in a fine house down in the mud."

"Croak, croak, ribit!" was all the son said. Then they took the pretty little walnut bed and carried it off.

Poor Thumbelina sat alone on the lily pad and cried. She did not want to live with the ugly old toad or marry her horrible son. The little fishes who were

8

swimming around in the water had heard what the old toad said, so they poked their heads out of the water to get a look at Thumbelina. When they saw her, they were amazed by her beauty. It pained them to think she'd have to live in the mud with the toads.

"We will not let that happen!" they declared. Then all the little fishes dived back under the water. They gathered around the green stalk that held the lily pad in place and quickly gnawed through it with their teeth. Both the lily pad and the little girl were carried away by the flowing stream to where the toads could never reach her.

Thumbelina sailed farther and farther down the stream, and whenever the birds on the shore saw her

pass, they sang happily, "Come look! What a lovely little girl!"

The lily pad drifted with the current for many days, until at last, it reached another country. A lovely white butterfly fluttered round and round, and finally it settled on the lily pad. It had taken a liking to Thumbelina. And the little girl laughed because the toads couldn't reach her and because the brook was so beautiful. The sun shone on the water like sparkling gold. Thumbelina took the sash from around her waist and tied one end around the butterfly. The other she fixed to the lily pad so that now it glided on much faster than before.

Just then, a large beetle flew past, and when he

saw Thumbelina, he swooped down. He put his claws around her tiny waist and carried her up into a tree. The lily pad went sailing on, and the butterfly went with it.

My gosh, how it frightened Thumbelina to be carried away by the beetle! But worse than that, she worried about the poor little butterfly she had tied to the lily pad. Unless it could free itself, it would surely starve to death! The beetle didn't care about the butterfly, though. He set Thumbelina down on the highest part of the tree. He gave her honey from a flower to eat and told her she was lovely, even though she didn't look like a beetle.

Soon all the other beetles that lived on the tree came to visit. They stared at Thumbelina, and two young lady beetles wiggled their feelers and said, "Why, she's got only two legs! How awful. And she has no feelers!"

"How narrow her waist is!" the others exclaimed. "Ewww! She looks just like a human! How ugly!" The stag beetle thought Thumbelina was very lovely—and she was. But when all the others kept saying how ugly she was, he began to think he was mistaken.

Now he didn't want her, so he carried her down from the tree and sat her on a daisy. He told her that she could go wherever she wanted. And Thumbelina wept to think she was so ugly that even the beetles wouldn't have her.

That whole summer, Thumbelina lived all alone in the great forest. She wove herself a bed from blades of grass, and hung it under a dock leaf for shelter from the rain. She ate honey from the flowers and drank morning dew from the leaves. So summer passed, and

autumn, too. And now came the long, cold winter.

All the birds that had sung so beautifully flew away. The trees grew bare and the flowers withered. Thumbelina was so cold! Her clothes were in tatters, and she was such a delicate, tiny thing that she was bound to freeze to death. Then it started to snow, and each snowflake felt like a shovelful landing on one of us. Thumbelina wrapped herself in a dried leaf, but it

couldn't keep her warm as she wandered through the forest.

At the edge of the forest lay a large cornfield, but the corn had long been cut. Now there was only dry stubble sticking up from the frozen earth.

At last, she came to a field mouse's home, a hole beneath the corn stubble, where the mouse was warm and snug. She had a roomful of corn and a fine kitchen. Poor Thumbelina stood like a beggar at the door and asked for a bit of barleycorn. She hadn't eaten a thing in the past two days.

"You poor little thing!" said the field mouse, for she was really a kindhearted creature. "Do come into my warm little house and have dinner with me."

The field mouse liked Thumbelina, so she said, "You can spend the winter here with me, if you'll keep my house tidy and tell me stories. You see, I am very fond of stories." Of course, Thumbelina agreed at once, and so she lived happily with the field mouse.

"Soon we shall have a visitor," said the mouse one day. "My neighbor visits once a week. He is even more comfortable than I. He has larger rooms, and he wears such a lovely black velvet coat! Ah, if only you could marry him, you would be so very well off! You must tell him the best stories you know, for that will delight him, I'm sure."

Thumbelina did not want to marry the neighbor, for he was a mole. He wore his black velvet coat when

he came calling the next day. The field mouse had said he was both rich and wise. And he was very learned, but he couldn't bear the sun or the lovely bright flowers. He had never seen them, and he spoke badly of them.

Thumbelina had to sing for him, and when she sang *Ladybug, ladybug, fly away home,* the mole fell in love with her because she had such a beautiful voice. But he said nothing about it, because he was a cautious fellow.

The mole had recently dug a long passage from his house to theirs. Now he invited them to walk there whenever they pleased. He told them not to be afraid of the dead bird in the passage, for it was still whole.

It must have died when winter began, and now it was buried right inside the passage.

The mole took a piece of touchwood, for in the dark, it glows like fire. Then he led the way through the passage. When they came to the spot where the bird lay, the mole raised his big snout to the ceiling and moved some earth making a large hole that let in some daylight. In the middle of the passage lay the dead swallow. Its pretty wings were folded shut, and its head and claws were hidden under its feathers. The poor bird must have died from the cold.

Thumbelina felt so sorry for the swallow! She loved all the birds that had twittered and sung so sweetly all summer. But the mole kicked it aside with

17

his stumpy legs and said, "At least he's not making a racket anymore! It must be a wretched thing to be born a bird. Thank goodness none of my children will be birds! They do nothing but twitter and chirp, and then they freeze to death when winter comes."

"Yes, you are very sensible," said the field mouse. "What good is all that chirping and singing? When winter comes along, you starve and freeze. But I suppose they think it's noble."

Thumbelina didn't say anything, but when the other two turned their backs, she bent down and smoothed the feathers that lay on the swallow's head. Then she kissed its closed eyelids. Perhaps it was you who sang so sweetly to me all summer," she whispered. "And how much pleasure you gave me!"

Now the mole closed up the hole he had made and shut out all the daylight. Then he took Thumbelina and the mouse back to their home. That night, Thumbelina couldn't sleep, so she got up and made a large blanket out of hay. She carried it down to the passage and spread it gently over the dead bird. She had found some fine down in the mouse's home, and she wrapped this all around the swallow so it would be warm in the cold earth.

"Goodbye, you beautiful bird," she said. "Thank you for the sweet songs you sang last summer, when the trees were green and the sun warmed us both!"

Thumbelina laid her head down on the swallow's breast. Then she jumped in surprise—something was beating inside! It was the swallow's heart. For he was not really dead, but just numb with cold. Now that it was warmer, the bird revived. In fall, the swallows fly to the warmer countries. But if one of them stays behind too long, it gets so cold that it falls to the ground as if dead. Then it lies there until the snow buries it.

Thumbelina gathered her courage and tucked more down around the swallow. Then she ran to get the woven leaves she had been using as a blanket, and she spread this over the bird's head.

The next night she crept back to the passage to see the swallow. He was alive, but so weak he could hardly open his eyes. Still, he saw Thumbelina standing there with a piece of glowing wood.

"Thank you, lovely child," whispered the sick swallow. "I am so nice and warm now. I shall soon be

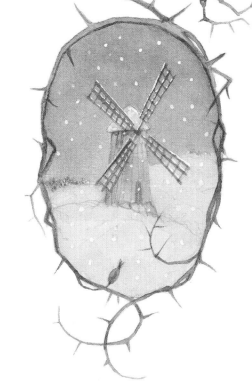

strong enough to fly out in the warm sunshine again."

"Oh, no!" said Thumbelina. "Right now it is cold outside. You must stay in your warm bed. I will take care of you." Thumbelina brought him water on a leaf, and after he drank it, the swallow told his story.

He had torn his wing on a thornbush, so he couldn't fly as fast as the other swallows when they left for the warmer countries. He flew alone for a long time. Then he fell to the ground. That was all he could remember. He had no idea how he came to be in the passage.

The bird stayed underground all winter. Thumbelina took care of him and grew very fond of him. She never said a word about him to the mole or the field mouse, for she knew they didn't like birds.

As soon as spring came and the sun warmed the earth, the swallow opened up the hole that the mole had made in the roof. The glorious sunshine poured into the passage and the swallow asked Thumbelina if she would like to fly away with him. She could sit on his back, and they would fly far out into the green forest.

But Thumbelina knew it would make the field mouse sad to be left alone that way. So she sighed, and said, "No, I cannot come."

"Good-by, then, you dear girl," said the swallow. And he flew up into the sunshine. Thumbelina gazed after him with her eyes full of tears.

"Tweet, tweet!" sang the bird as he flew off toward the green forest. Poor Thumbelina sadly remained behind. She was never allowed out in the warm light of the sun, and soon the corn, which was planted in the field above the field mouse's home, would seem as high to her as a towering forest.

"This summer, you must prepare your wedding clothes," said the field mouse one day. The boring old mole with his black velvet fur coat had asked for Thumbelina's hand in marriage. "You must have things of wool and linen, for only the finest is good enough for the wedding outfit of a mole's bride!"

Thumbelina had to work very hard at her spindle to make wool and linen outfits. The mouse even hired four spiders to work night and day as weavers. Every evening the mole came around to visit, and he always said the same thing: when the summer was over and the the sun no longer baked the ground as hard as rock, they would celebrate their marriage.

Thumbelina, meanwhile, was very unhappy, for

she did not like the tiresome mole at all. Every morning when the sun rose, and every evening when it set, she would slip out the door. When the wind blew aside the ears of corn so that she could catch a glimpse of the blue sky, she would think how lovely it was out in the open, and she longed to see her dear swallow again. But he never came back, for by this time he was flying far away in the beautiful green forest.

When fall came, Thumbelina was very unhappy. She cried and said she would not marry the mole.

"Nonsense," said the field mouse. "You have found a fine husband with a lovely black velvet coat and both a cellar and a kitchen. You ought to be grateful for your good fortune."

At last the wedding day came. The mole came to take Thumbelina deep under the earth. Never again would she go out into the sunshine, for the mole didn't like it.

Thumbelina was heartbroken. "Good-by, bright sun!" she said, and lifted her arms up high.

"Good-by, good-by!" she cried again. Then she threw her arms around a little red flower that grew nearby. "Give my love to the dear swallow, if you ever happen to see him!"

"Tweet, Tweet!" At that moment, Thumbelina heard a chattering noise above her head. She looked up, and there was the swallow passing by. As soon as he saw her, he flew to her, chirping with delight. She told him that she was about to be married to the boring old mole. They would live forever under the ground where the sun never shone. Just telling him was enough to make her cry again.

"The cold winter is coming soon," said the swallow, "and I must fly to the warmer countries. Will you come with me? You can climb onto my back. Just tie yourself on with your sash, and we'll fly away from the mole and his gloomy house. We'll go where the sun shines more brightly than it does here. There are always flowers, and summer never ends. Come with me, Thumbelina, for you saved my life when I lay frozen in the cold earth!"

"Yes, I will come with you!" said Thumbelina. She climbed onto the swallow's back and rested her feet on his open wings. Then she fastened her sash to the bird's strongest feathers. The swallow flew high up into the sky, over rivers, lakes and great snow-capped mountains. Thumbelina was freezing in the cold air. But then she nestled in under the bird's warm feathers,

and only her head peeped out to admire the lovely lands below.

By and by, they came to the warm countries, where the sun shone more brightly than it does here, and the sky looked twice as high. On fences and hillsides grew the finest green and purple grapes. From the trees hung oranges and lemons. The air smelled sweetly of myrtle and mint. Children ran along chasing butterflies of every color.

At last they came to the shore of a blue lake near a great green forest. There stood an ancient palace made of pure white marble. Ivy went up the tall pillars, and at the top were the nests of many birds. One of them was home to the swallow.

"This is where I live," he said. "Now you can choose one of those beautiful flowers for yourself. I will set you down on it, and you shall have everything you need."

"Oh, how lovely!" said Thumbelina.

On the ground lay a white marble pillar in pieces, and between the pieces grew pretty white flowers. The swallow flew down and placed Thumbelina on one— and what a surprise she got! In the middle of the flower sat a tiny man as light and clear as glass. He wore a gold crown on his head and a pair of bright wings on his shoulders, for he was the spirit of the flower. Every flower held such a little man or woman inside, and he was king of them all.

"He is so handsome!" cried Thumbelina.

At first, the little king was frightened of the swallow, for it seemed like a giant to him. But when he saw Thumbelina, he was delighted. She was the loveliest girl he had ever seen. He placed his gold crown on her head and asked her to marry him and become queen of the flowers.

Now this was a proper husband! Thumbelina said yes, and a lovely spirit came from every flower to bring her gifts. The best one of all was a pair of pearly wings, which were fastened to her shoulders. Now she, too, could fly!

It was a day of joy, and the swallow sang for them, though he was sad to leave her.

"You shall no longer be called Thumbelina," said the flower king. "It is an ugly name, and you are lovely. We will call you Maia, Queen of the Flowers."

"Good-by," sang the swallow, as he flew back to Denmark. There he built a nest near a man who told fairy tales. "Tweet, tweet, tweet," he sang to the man.   And that's how we know this story.

28

The Tinderbox

A soldier came marching along the road: Left, right! Left, right! He had a knapsack on his back and a sword at his side, for he had been in the war. Now he was returning home. On the road, he met an old witch—a horrible, ugly old creature.

"Good evening, soldier," she said. "What a nice sword and what a big knapsack! I can see that you are a true soldier. I will give you all the money you could want."

"Thank you very much, old witch," said the soldier.

"Do you see that big tree over there?" said the witch, pointing to the tree next to them. "It is hollow inside. Climb up the tree and you will find a hole. Slip through it and lower yourself deep down in the tree. I will tie a rope around your waist so I can pull you up again when you call me."

"But what am I to do down in the tree?" asked the soldier.

"Fetch money!" said the witch. "Listen. When you get to the bottom of the tree, you'll be in a great, lighted hall. You will see three doors, and you can open them all, for the keys are in the locks.

"When you go in the first room, you'll see a large chest with a dog sitting on it. He has eyes as big as saucers. But never mind about that: I will give you my blue-checked apron. Spread it out on the floor, then go briskly to the dog and put him on the apron. Open the chest and take as much money as you wish.

"It is all copper, but if you would rather have silver, then go to the next room. There is a dog with eyes as big as mill wheels, but never mind about that. Just put him down on my apron and take the money from the chest.

"However, if you want gold, just go into the third room. The dog that sits on that chest has eyes as big as the Round Tower in Copenhagen. It's some dog! But never mind about that. Just put him on my apron, and he won't hurt you. Then you can take as much gold as you like."

"That doesn't sound bad!" said the soldier. "But what do you want in return, old witch?"

"I don't want a single penny," said the witch. "Just bring me an old tinderbox for lighting fires that my grandmother forgot last time she was down there."

"Very well," said the soldier. "Tie that rope around my waist!"

"Here it is," she said. "And here is my apron."

The soldier climbed up the tree and let himself fall down into the hole. At the bottom, he found himself standing in a great hall, ablaze with light, just

30

as the witch had said. The soldier opened the first door. There sat the dog with eyes as big as saucers, glaring at him.

"Good dog!" said the soldier. And he picked him up and put him on the witch's blue-checked apron. Then he filled his pockets with copper pennies, shut the chest, and put the dog back on top.

Next, he went into the second room. My word! There sat the dog with eyes as big as mill wheels.

"You really shouldn't stare like that," said the soldier. "You will hurt your eyes." And when he saw all the silver coins in the chest, he hastily removed the dog and placed it on the apron. Then the soldier threw away the copper pennies and filled his pockets and his knapsack with silver.

Now he went into the third room. Oh, no! The third dog really did have eyes as big as the Round Tower, and they rolled in his head like wheels!

"Good evening," said the soldier, and he tipped his cap, for he had never seen a dog like that before. But after he studied it awhile, he said to himself,

"Enough of this!" He lifted the huge dog onto the apron and opened up the chest.

Oh, my gosh! What a lot of gold there was! There was enough to buy the whole city of Copenhagen, and all the gingerbread men, tin soldiers, riding whips, and rocking horses in the world. The soldier quickly threw away the silver and filled his pockets and backpack with gold. Then he filled up his cap and boots until he could hardly walk with the weight he carried. He put the dog back onto the chest, shut the door of the room behind him, and shouted up through the hollow tree, "Pull me up now, old witch!"

"Have you got the tinderbox?" she asked.

"Oh, I forgot!" said the soldier. So he went back

to fetch the box. Then the witch pulled him up, and he was standing there loaded with gold.

"What are you going to do with the tinderbox?" he asked.

"None of your business!" said the witch.

"Nonsense," said the soldier. "Either you tell me right now what you want with the tinderbox, or I will take out my sword and cut your head off!"

"No. I won't tell you!" said the witch. And the soldier did cut her head off then. There she lay! Then the soldier wrapped up all his money in the blue-checked apron and slung it across his back. He put the tinderbox in his pocket and trudged off toward the nearest city.

It was a fine city, and the soldier stayed at the finest inn. He asked for the best room and all the foods he liked most, for at last he was a rich man.

The next day he went out and bought good boots and smart clothes, and then he became a fine gentleman. People were glad to talk with him about the city, the king, and the beautiful princess who was the king's daughter.

"I really would like to see her," said the soldier.

"It is absolutely impossible to see the princess!" they told him. "She lives in a great copper castle surrounded by walls and towers. It was foretold that a common soldier would marry her, and the king hates the idea."

The soldier now lived a merry life. He went to the theater, drove in the royal parks, and gave a great deal of money to the poor. He remembered well how wretched it was not to have a penny in one's pocket. But now he was rich and well dressed, so he had lots of friends who told him what a fine gentleman he was.

All this pleased the soldier greatly. But as he kept on giving and spending every day, and never receiving anything, he was finally left with only a few cents. Now he had to leave his beautiful room and go to live in a poor garret. He had to shine and mend his boots himself. And none of his friends ever came to see him, because there were so many stairs to climb!

One evening it was very dark, and the soldier couldn't even buy a candle. Then he remembered the bit of candle in the tinderbox he'd got from the witch. As soon as he struck the box, a spark flew up. The door opened, and there stood the dog who has eyes as big as saucers.

"What does my lord command?" growled the dog.

"Without a doubt, this must be a magic tinderbox," thought the soldier, "if I can have anything I want." So he said to the dog, "Go fetch me some money!" The creature vanished, but in an instant returned with a large bag of copper pennies in his mouth.

Now the soldier began to understand the magic of the tinderbox. If he struck it once, the dog who sat on the chest full of copper came to him. If he struck it twice, the dog who guarded the silver came. And if he struck it three times, there came the dog who guarded the gold.

So the soldier went back to live in his fine room, and wore elegant clothes once more. All his friends

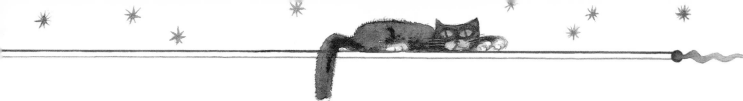

recognized him again and said how highly they thought of him.

One night the soldier thought how unfair it was that no one could see the princess. Everyone said she was beautiful. But what was the good of her beauty if she had to stay in the copper castle?

"There must be a way to see her," he said. "Now where is my tinderbox?" The soldier struck the box once and there stood the dog with eyes as big as saucers.

"I know it is the middle of the night," said the soldier, "but I would like to see the beautiful princess, if only for a moment."

The dog vanished, and in the blink of an eye, it returned with the sleeping princess on its back. She was so lovely that anyone could tell she was a true princess. And the soldier could not help himself: He had to kiss her.

Then the dog carried the princess back to the great copper castle. But the next morning, while she had breakfast with the king and queen, the princess said she'd had such a strange dream! A big dog had come and carried her away, and a soldier had kissed her.

"That's a pretty dream!" said the queen. And that night she told one of the old ladies in waiting to watch

over the princess at night to find out if it was really a dream, or something else.

The same evening, the soldier longed to see the princess again, so he sent the dog to fetch her. The dog was fast as ever, but the old lady ran just as fast. When she saw the dog enter a large house, she thought, "I know what to do!" And with a piece of chalk she drew a large white cross on the door. Then she went home to bed.

When the dog carried the princess back to the castle, he saw the cross drawn on the door of the soldier's house. So he took some chalk and made a white cross on every door in the city. Now this was a clever thing to do. The old lady would never find the right place!

The next morning, the king and queen, the old lady, and the court officials went to see where the princess had been.

"Here it is!" said the king, when he saw the first door with a cross on it.

"No, dear husband, there it is!" said the queen.

"Here is another! There is another!" cried all the court officials. Wherever they looked, they found a door with a cross on it. So then they gave up their search.

But the queen was a clever woman who could do more than ride smartly in a carriage. She took her great golden scissors, cut a big piece of silk, and made a pretty little bag. She filled it with flour and tied it around the princess's waist. Now it would leave a trail wherever the princess went.

That night the dog came and carried the princess to the soldier. By now, he loved her so much that he wanted only to be a prince so he could marry her. But this time, the dog did not notice the trail of flour

that fell all along the way from the castle as far as the soldier's window, which he entered with the beautiful princess. The next morning, the king and queen could see where the princess had been. So they had the soldier seized and thrown into prison.

There he sat. How dark and dreary it was! The guards kept telling him he would be hanged in the morning. The soldier was in a hopeless situation, and worse, he had left his tinderbox at the inn.

In the morning, the soldier looked out the tiny prison window. He could see people rushing to the city gates to watch him hang. Among the crowd was a shoemaker's apprentice, wearing a leather apron and a pair of slippers. He was running so fast that one of his slippers fell off and struck the very bars of the prison window.

"Hey, little apprentice!" called the soldier. "There's no need to be in such a hurry. They can't start without me! If you will run to my room and fetch my tinderbox, I will give you two pennies. But run as fast as you can!"

The boy was keen to earn the money, so away he raced to get the tinderbox, which he carried back to the soldier. And just listen to what happened next!

Outside the city gates a gallows had been built on a high platform, and around it stood soldiers and thousands of people. The king and queen sat on their royal thrones, and below them sat the judge and the entire council. The soldier was already on the platform, and the rope was being put around his neck, when he called out that a condemned man was always granted a harmless last request before being executed. All he wanted, he said, was to smoke a last pipe of tobacco since he would never be able to smoke another.

The king could not refuse him, so the soldier struck his tinderbox once, twice, three times! Instantly, all three dogs stood there: one with eyes as big as saucers, one with eyes as big as mill wheels, and one with eyes as big as the Round Tower of Copenhagen.

"Help me now! Don't let me be hanged!" cried the soldier to the dogs. At these words, the terrible dogs threw themselves on the judge and the entire

council, tossing them so high in the air they were dashed to pieces when they fell.

"No, not me!" cried the king, but the dogs threw him and the queen even higher than the rest.

The soldiers and the crowd were so terrified, that with one voice they shouted, "Good soldier! You shall be our king and our beautiful princess shall be your wife and queen!"

Then they begged the soldier to be seated in the king's carriage, while the dogs jumped for joy. The crowd cheered and the soldiers saluted. The princess left her castle and became queen. The wedding celebration lasted for a week, and the magic dogs were given places at the royal table, where they sat staring around with their great eyes!

The Steadfast Tin Soldier

Once there were twenty-five tin soldiers. They were all brothers, made from the same old tin spoon. They carried muskets in their arms and stood at attention with heads held high. Their uniforms were of blue, white and red, very fine indeed. The first words they heard in this world, when the lid was removed from their box, were "Tin soldiers!" A little boy shouted the words and clapped his hands in delight. The soldiers were a present for his birthday, and now he lined them up on the table.

All the soldiers were exactly the same, except for one. He had only one leg because he had been made last, when there was not quite enough tin left. Yet he stood as firmly on one leg as the others did on two. And it is of him that our story tells.

On the table with the soldiers were many other toys, but the one you noticed first was a castle of painted cardboard. You could look through its tiny windows right into the rooms. In front, tiny trees surrounded a little mirror that stood for a lake. Little wax swans swam there, gazing at their own reflections. And prettiest of all was a little lady who stood in the open doorway of the castle.

She, too, was cardboard but wore a dress of the finest silk. A pale blue ribbon was draped about her shoulder and held by a sequin, a glittering jewel as big as her face. The lady held out both her arms in a graceful pose, for she was a ballerina. She kept one leg raised so high that the soldier could not see it. So he thought she had only one leg, like him.

"She would be the perfect wife for me!" he thought. "But she must be a lady of high rank. She lives in a castle, and I live in a box with twenty-four other soldiers. That's no place for her! Still, I would like to meet her." Then he positioned himself behind a snuff box on the table. From there he could gaze at the beautiful lady who stood on one leg without losing her balance.

That night all the other tin soldiers were put back in the box, and the people of the house went to bed. Then the toys began to play. They played house, and had battles, and held a ball. The tin soldiers rattled in their box because they wanted to play, but they could not get the lid off their box.

The nutcrackers turned somersaults, and the chalk danced noisily on the chalkboard. There was such a racket that the canary woke up and began to sing—in verse! The only ones who didn't move were the tin soldier and the little ballerina. She kept standing on tiptoe, with her arms outstretched. He, no less firm, stood upright on his one leg. His eyes never left her for a moment.

Then the clock struck twelve and—*pop!*—the lid of the snuff box flew open— the box was really a jack-in-the-box. Out jumped a little black goblin.

"Tin soldier!" cried the goblin, "Please keep your eyes to yourself!"

The tin soldier pretended not to hear.

"Just wait until tomorrow, then!" threatened the little goblin.

When tomorrow came, the little children got up, and they moved the tin soldier to the window ledge.

All of a sudden—whether the goblin or the wind caused it—the window flew open, and the tin soldier fell out, head first, from the third floor! He fell at a frightening speed, with his leg pointing up in the air. He landed on his head, his bayonet stuck between two cobblestones.

The maid and the little boy ran downstairs to look for him. Though they nearly stepped on him, they didn't see him. If only he would have called out, "Here I am!" they would have found him easily. But the tin soldier didn't think it was proper to cry out while in uniform.

It began to rain, one drop after another, until it was a perfect downpour. When it stopped, two boys came by. "Look at that!" said one of them. "It's a tin soldier! Let's send him on a fine trip!"

The boys made a boat out of newspaper and put the little tin soldier on board. Away he sailed, down

the gutter, while the boys ran along, clapping their hands. Good heavens! What waves there were in the gutter, and what a strong current there was! Truly, it was a flood! The paper boat whirled around so fast that the tin soldier felt completely dizzy. Still, he remained steadfast, keeping his musket on his shoulder and looking straight ahead.

Suddenly the boat slipped into a long underground canal. It was completely dark there.

"Where on earth am I going?" thought the soldier. "I am sure this is all the fault of that goblin! If only the ballerina were here with me now, I wouldn't care if it were twice as dark!"

Just then, a great big water rat leaped out of the gutter. "Where is your passport?" he screeched. "To travel here, you must have a passport!"

But the tin soldier didn't say a word. He just held his musket more tightly than ever.

The boat sailed on, and the rat chased after it. Oh, how it gnashed its teeth! It cried out to all the sticks and straws, "Stop him! Stop him! He hasn't paid the toll! He hasn't even shown his passport!"

Meanwhile, the current was growing stronger and stronger, and at last the tin soldier saw a glimmer of daylight ahead. But he also began to hear a roar that would make the bravest person tremble. At the end of the tunnel, the water fell a long way down to a great canal. For the tin soldier, this danger was as great as it would be for us to go over a waterfall. But he was already so close that he couldn't stop. When the boat plunged over the edge, the poor soldier held himself as stiff as possible. No one could say that he showed any sign of fear.

The boat spun around three—no, four—times, and filled with water until it could do nothing but sink. The tin soldier stayed upright as the water reached his neck, the wet paper began to tear, and the water went over his head. Then the tin soldier thought of the graceful little ballerina he would never see again, and he said to himself:

> *Onward, onward, soldier brave,*
> *Each of us must face the grave!*

The paper boat fell apart, and the tin soldier sank down . . . and was instantly swallowed up by a large fish! How dark it was inside the fish. It was even darker than the tunnel, and much more cramped! But the tin soldier was not discouraged. He lay as straight as ever, his musket on his shoulder.

After a time, the fish began to twist and thrash about in a terrifying way, but at last it lay still. There came a flash of light. Daylight blazed, and someone cried, "The tin soldier!"

50

The fish had been caught, taken to market, and sold. In the kitchen, the cook had cut it open. Now she picked up the soldier with two fingers and carried him into the living room. There everyone wished to see the hero who had traveled in the belly of a fish. But the tin soldier was not boastful.

They set him on the table, and . . . what a strange world it is! The tin soldier found himself in the room he had left before. He saw the same children

and the same toys. There were the castle and the graceful little ballerina who still stood on one leg. She had been steadfast, too!

The tin soldier was so touched he would have cried, only he thought it was not fitting for a soldier to weep. He looked at the dancer and she looked at him, but neither one spoke a word.

Suddenly one of the children grabbed the tin soldier and threw him into the stove. The child had no reason for doing it, so it must have been the work of the goblin.

The tin soldier found himself in a great light and felt a suffocating heat, but he did not know whether the cause was the heat of the fire or of his warm love. He had lost his colors—whether from his travels or from grief he could not tell.

For the last time, he looked at the ballerina and she looked at him. He felt himself melting, yet he still stood straight, his musket on his shoulder.

Then a door opened and a gust of wind caught the ballerina. She flew like a sylph into the fire, to join the soldier. She flared up in flame and was gone. Then the tin soldier melted away.

The next day, when the maid cleaned out the grate, she found what remained of the tin soldier: a little tin heart. Nothing remained of the dancer but her sequin, and that was burned as black as coal. The heart and the sequin lay as close as the love between the tin soldier and the little ballerina.

The Emperor's New Clothes

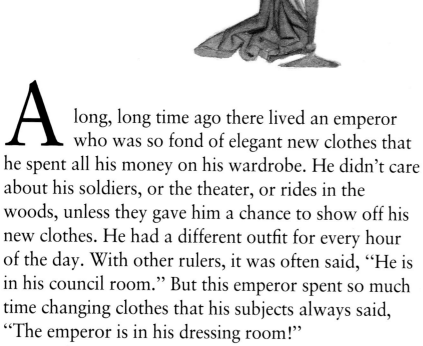

A long, long time ago there lived an emperor who was so fond of elegant new clothes that he spent all his money on his wardrobe. He didn't care about his soldiers, or the theater, or rides in the woods, unless they gave him a chance to show off his new clothes. He had a different outfit for every hour of the day. With other rulers, it was often said, "He is in his council room." But this emperor spent so much time changing clothes that his subjects always said, "The emperor is in his dressing room!"

In the great city where the emperor kept his court, life was busy. Every day strangers arrived, and among them were some rogues. One day it became known that two master weavers had arrived. It was said that they were able to weave the most extraordinary cloth imaginable. Not only were its colors and designs of incomparable beauty, but the cloth also had a marvelous power: it was invisible to

all those who were unfit for their offices or were particularly stupid.

"I absolutely must have an outfit made from that cloth," thought the emperor. "By wearing it, I could discover which of my subjects are unfit for their posts. In addition, I could tell the wise people from the foolish!" Therefore the emperor sent a large sum of money to the swindlers so that they could begin work.

The men set up two looms and made a great show of working, but the looms held absolutely nothing. Impudently, the rogues asked for the finest silks and the purest gold thread, which they put straight into their knapsacks. They went on pretending to work on the looms until late each night.

"I wonder how the weavers are getting on with my cloth," thought the emperor after a while. But then he remembered that stupid or incompetent people would not be able to see the cloth. That made him hesitate to make the inspection himself. He was sure he had nothing to fear. Nevertheless, he preferred to send someone else.

All the citizens had heard of the miraculous cloth and waited impatiently to find out just how stupid and incompetent their neighbors were.

"I will send my honest old minister to the weavers," the emperor decided at last. "He is the

person best qualified to judge the quality of the cloth. He is a man of good sense, and nobody is more fit for office than he."

So the faithful old minister went to the room where the two rogues were pretending to work at empty looms. "My word," he thought, staring hard, "I can see nothing at all!" But, naturally, he was careful not to say this aloud.

The impostors invited him to take a closer look. "Isn't the design perfect?" they asked. "Aren't the colors charming?" The poor old minister peered even more closely at the empty looms. Still, he could see nothing there, for the simple reason that there was nothing to see.

"Poor me!" thought the minister. "Is it possible that I am stupid? The idea never crossed my mind before, and it must not cross anyone else's mind now! Can it be that I am unfit for my office? No, that cannot be! I must never say that I cannot see the cloth!"

"You have not said if you like it . . ." said one of the rogues, still pretending to weave.

"Oh . . . yes, it's marvelous!" said the minister, putting on his spectacles. "What a design! What colors! Yes, I will be sure to tell the emperor I am immensely pleased."

"That is most kind of you!" replied the weavers. Then they began describing the colors and unusual quality of the cloth. The old minister listened carefully, so that he could repeat their exact words to the emperor. And that is just what he did.

Then the rogues asked for more supplies of money, of silk, and of gold thread, which they needed, they said, to continue their work. Instead, they put everything into their knapsacks. Not even a thread

reached the empty loom where they pretended to work.

After a while, the emperor sent another trusted official to judge how the work was going. He wanted to know whether the clothes would be ready soon. The same thing happened to the second official as to the first. He looked and looked but, since the looms were empty, could not see a thing.

"Beautiful, isn't it?" asked the rogues, showing him the cloth and explaining the marvelous design that wasn't there.

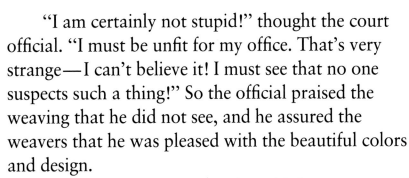

"I am certainly not stupid!" thought the court official. "I must be unfit for my office. That's very strange—I can't believe it! I must see that no one suspects such a thing!" So the official praised the weaving that he did not see, and he assured the weavers that he was pleased with the beautiful colors and design.

"Indeed, Your Majesty," he told the emperor, "it is the most beautiful cloth I ever saw!"

By now, the splendid cloth was the talk of the town. So the emperor decided to see it while it was still on the loom. Accompanied by a crowd of courtiers, including the two officials who had already been there, he went to visit the swindlers. They were

busily weaving with great energy, but without warp or woof.

"Isn't it magnificent?" asked the two old officials. "Observe, Your Majesty. What a design! What colors!" And they pointed to the empty loom, convinced that everyone else could see the cloth.

"What is going on here?" thought the emperor. "I can't see anything. This is terrible! Am I stupid? Am I unfit to be emperor? That would be intolerable." Aloud, he said, "Oh, how beautiful! I approve of it entirely."

The emperor smiled with satisfaction at the empty loom, for nothing in the world would make him admit that he saw nothing.

All the courtiers looked and looked again, but not one of them could see a thing. Nevertheless, they all repeated in chorus with the emperor, "How marvelous! How marvelous!" And they advised the emperor to have a complete outfit made, to wear in the great procession that was coming soon.

"That cloth is excellent!" they said to each other. "Superb!" And they all seemed genuinely impressed. So the emperor conferred a knighthood on each of the rogues, giving them the title of Knights of the Loom.

The night before the big procession, the two swindlers worked until dawn. They set sixteen candles burning in the window, so everyone could see how hard they were working. They pretended to lift the cloth from the loom. With large scissors they cut ample pieces of . . . air. They sewed with empty needles. And, at last, they cried, "Look! The emperor's robes are complete!"

Accompanied by his most important courtiers, the emperor went to be fitted. The two impostors raised their arms as if holding up something and said, "Here are the breeches and tights, this is the jacket, here is the mantle," and so on.

"The whole outfit is as light as a cobweb, Your Majesty," they exclaimed. "You will feel as if you were wearing nothing at all."

"Oh, yes!" breathed the courtiers, though none of them could see a thing. After all, there was nothing to be seen!

"And now, if Your Majesty would be gracious enough to undress?" asked the swindlers. "We shall be pleased to fit you with your new robes here in front of this mirror."

So the emperor took off his clothes, and the rogues pretended to dress him, garment by garment.

Finally, they pretended to tie a belt around his waist. Then they stood back while the emperor turned from side to side in front of the mirror.

"How regal you look, Your Majesty!" cried the courtiers. "What a wonderful fit! The style and colors are a marvel! A truly precious cloth!"

Then the master of ceremonies arrived. "The canopy to be held over Your Majesty has arrived," he said. "It is waiting in the square."

"Very well," said the emperor. "I am ready. My

new clothes fit well, don't they?" And he pretended to check the mirror one more time.

The lords-in-waiting fumbled about on the ground, pretending to pick up the train they couldn't see. Then they lined up behind the emperor with their hands raised, being careful not to let anyone know that they saw nothing.

Then the emperor began his march, walking beneath his rich canopy. The crowd in the streets and at the windows remarked, "Goodness! Look at the emperor's new clothes. No one has ever seen the like. Look at the marvelous train. What a perfect fit!" No one wanted anyone else to think that he or she couldn't see the clothes, for fear of being thought stupid. Never had a royal outfit met with such success.

"But he hasn't got any clothes on!" said a little child.

"Listen to the voice of innocence!" exclaimed the child's father.

And everyone began to repeat the child's words.

"He has no clothes on! A child said it. The emperor isn't wearing any clothes!"

Very soon the whole crowd was shouting, "The emperor isn't wearing any clothes!" And the emperor realized that the crowd was right. But he thought to himself, "I must carry on to the end, or the parade will be ruined." So he drew himself up more proudly than before, while the lords-in-waiting followed, carrying a train that wasn't there.

The Swineherd

There once was a poor prince who had only a very small kingdom. Still, his kingdom was large enough to support a family, so the prince decided to marry. Now, it was awfully bold of him to propose to the emperor's daughter, but the prince's name and valor were known far and wide. At least a hundred princesses would have married him gladly. But what about the emperor's daughter? Well, let's see.

In the grave of the prince's father, there grew a rose tree. And what a lovely tree! It blossomed only once every five years, and then it produced only a single bloom. But the rose that bloomed was so sweet that those who smelled it forgot their cares and sorrows. The prince also had a nightingale that poured from its throat the world's sweetest melodies. The rose and the nightingale were to be the prince's gifts to the emperor's daughter. So he put them into little golden caskets and had them sent to her.

The emperor had the gifts brought into the great hall, where the princess was playing court with her maids of honor. It was the only game they ever played. When she saw the little golden caskets, the princess clapped her hands with joy.

"Oh, I do hope there is a kitten in one of them!" she exclaimed. But then the beautiful rose was brought out.

"How pretty it is!" cried the ladies of the court.

"It is more than pretty, it is perfect," declared the emperor. But when the princess touched it, she was so disappointed.

"Oh, horrible, father!" she cried. "It is not artificial at all. It is just a real rose! How shameful!"

"How horrible!" echoed the maids of honor. "It is only a real rose!"

"Before we lose our tempers," said the emperor, "Let us see what is in the other casket."

And then out flew the nightingale. It sang so beautifully that, at first, no one could find any fault with it.

"Superbe! Charmant!" exclaimed the ladies, for they all spoke French—one worse than the other.

"That bird reminds me of the musical box of our dear, departed empress," said one old courtier with a sigh. "It has the same tone and the same expression."

"Yes, it does," agreed the emperor. And he began to weep like a baby.

"I hope it is not a real bird," said the princess.

"Why, yes. It is," replied one of the pages who had brought it.

"Well, then let it fly away." And she bluntly refused even to see the poor prince.

But the prince was not discouraged. He dabbed his face with mud, pulled his cap down over his eyes, and knocked on the castle door.

66

"Good day, mighty emperor," he said. "Can you give me a job at the palace?"

The emperor shook his head. "So many people come here looking for work," he sighed. "But let me see. . . I do need someone to take care of the pigs. We have so many pigs!"

So the prince was hired on as the imperial swineherd. He was given a dirty hut near the pigsties, and there he was obliged to live. He sat there all day and worked and by evening, he had made a fine little cooking pot with bells around the rim. Whenever the pot boiled, the bells would play:

> *Oh, my dearest Augustine,*
> *All is lost, lost, lost!*

But the cleverest thing about the pot was this: if you held your finger in the steam from the pot, you could smell the food cooking in every kitchen of the city. This was certainly a different matter from the sweet-smelling rose!

The princess was out walking with her maids of honor when she heard the music coming from the pot. She stopped, delighted, for she also could play "Dearest Augustine." It was the only musical piece she knew.

"Why, that's my piece!" the princess exclaimed. "That swineherd must be a very cultured fellow. Go ask him how much he wants for his musical instrument." So one of the ladies asked the swineherd,

"The princess would like to buy your pot. How much are you willing to sell it for?"

"Ten kisses from the princess," he replied.

"Goodness!" screeched the maid of honor.

"I won't take anything less," said the swineherd.

"What did he say?" asked the princess.

"It's too awful to repeat," said the maid.

"Then whisper it in my ear," said the princess. So the maid of honor whispered, and the princess gasped.

"What impudence!" she exclaimed, and she walked away. But she had gone only a few steps when the bells tinkled prettily again:

> *Oh, my dearest Augustine,*
> *All is lost, lost, lost!*

"Ask him," said the princess, "if he will accept ten kisses from my maids of honor."

"No, thank you!" replied the swineherd. "Ten kisses from the princess, or I keep my magic pot for myself."

"How insolent he is," sighed the princess to her maids. "You must all stand in front of me so that no one will see us." So the ladies of the court stood around the princess and spread out their dresses. Thus the swineherd got ten kisses and the princess got the musical pot.

And what fun it was! They made the pot boil all day and all night. Soon they knew what was cooking in every part of the city. The ladies danced and clapped their hands with glee. "We know who will eat soup and who will eat meat!" they squealed.

"Most interesting," observed the imperial cook.

"Yes, but don't tell anyone about this," warned the princess. "Remember, I am the emperor's daughter."

70

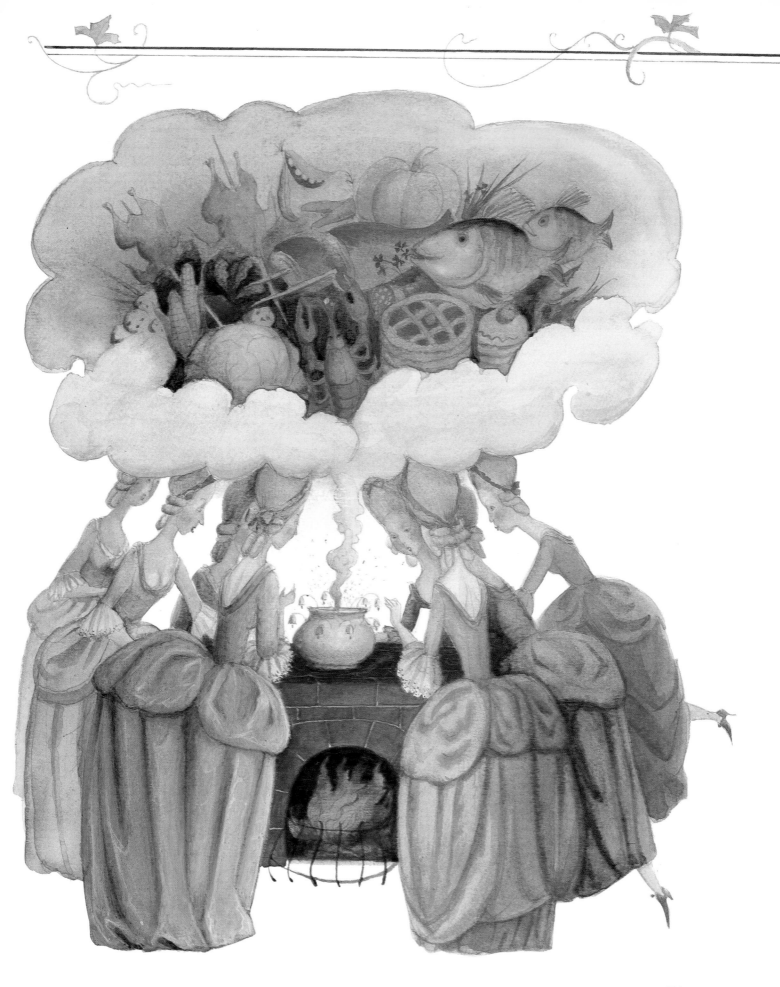

"Oh, of course!" cried the ladies of the court, in unison. "We won't say a word!"

The swineherd—that is, the prince they thought was a swineherd—made something new every day. One day he made a magic rattle. It played all the waltzes, polkas, and jigs that have ever been heard.

"How marvelous!" cried the princess when she walked by. "I have never heard such beautiful music. Go ask him the price of the instrument. But tell him, no more kisses!"

"He wants one hundred kisses from the princess!" said the maid of honor who had been sent to ask.

"He must be out of his mind!" exclaimed the princess, and she walked away. But after a few steps, she stopped and reflected: "We must encourage the fine arts," she said. "And I *am* the emperor's daughter. Tell him he shall have ten kisses from me. The others he will have from my maids of honor."

"Oh, but we would not like that!" objected the maids.

"Nonsense!" said the princess. "If I can kiss him, so can you. Don't forget that I am the emperor's daughter!" So the maid of honor returned to the swineherd.

"One hundred kisses from the princess," insisted the swineherd, "or I shall keep my musical rattle for myself."

"Gather round me again!" said the princess to her maids. And all the ladies stood around in a circle as the swineherd began to kiss the princess once more.

"Why is there such a big crowd at the pigsties?" wondered the emperor, who had just stepped out on his balcony. He rubbed his eyes and put on his glasses.

"Why," he exclaimed aloud, "it is the ladies of the court! They are up to some foolishness to be sure. I had better go see for myself."

The emperor pulled on his slippers, which were really just comfortable old shoes with the heels worn away. How comfortably he walked with them on his feet! When he arrived in the courtyard, he crept closer and stood on his tiptoes. But the ladies of the court did not notice the emperor. They were too busy counting kisses. They wanted to make sure the swineherd got neither too many nor too few.

"What is going on here?" the emperor shouted. He peered over the maids of honor for a better look.

Then he saw the kissing! He whacked the princess and the swineherd with his slipper, just as the swineherd was getting his eighty-sixth kiss.

"Be gone from my kingdom, the both of you!" he ordered. So both the princess and the swineherd were thrown out of the kingdom.

"Oh, poor me!" wailed the princess, trudging along with the swineherd. "If only I had married that handsome prince! How unhappy I am!"

The swineherd stepped behind a tree and cleaned the dirt from his face. Then he took off his filthy rags and stepped out in his princely robes. He looked so noble that the princess couldn't help but curtsy.

But the prince said, "I have learned to despise you! You rejected an honorable prince, and you did not appreciate the rose or the nightingale. Yet you were willing to kiss the swineherd for a silly musical toy. You have got what you deserve!"

The prince returned to his kingdom and shut the palace door in her face. The princess could only stand outside and sing:

> Oh, *my dearest Augustine,*
> *All is lost, lost, lost!*

The Nightingale of the Emperor

In China, as you know, the emperor is Chinese, and so are all his subjects. This story happened many years ago, and that is why you'd better hear it now, before it is forgotten.

The emperor's palace was the most beautiful palace in the whole world. It was made entirely of porcelain, and it was so fragile you had to be careful not to touch anything. The garden was full of lovely flowers with little silver bells attached. You couldn't pass by without noticing them.

Everything in the emperor's garden was most cleverly arranged. And the grounds stretched so far that not even the gardener knew where they ended. If you kept walking, you finally found a beautiful forest, with tall trees and broad lakes. The forest went on until it reached the sea, which was so deep and blue that even large ships could sail close to the shore and find shade under the trees.

Among these trees dwelt a nightingale. The bird sang so sweetly that even the poor fishermen, who were always full of worries when they came out to cast their nets in the evening, could not help but stop and listen.

"How beautiful," they exclaimed, before returning to work and forgetting about the bird. All the same, the very next evening the fishermen would stop work again to listen and exclaim: "How beautiful the nightingale sings!"

People came from all over the world to see the emperor's city, his palace, and his garden. But when they heard the nightingale, they all said the same thing: "Oh, but that bird is the best of all!"

When they returned from their travels, they would tell their tales. The most learned ones would write books about the emperor, his palace, and his garden. Yet they never forgot the nightingale. Poets even wrote beautiful verses about the nightingale who lived in the forest near the sea.

These books were read all over the world, and at last, one of them reached the emperor. He sat in his golden chair and began to read the book. Every so often, he nodded his head, for he was glad to read such wonderful descriptions of his city, his palace, and his garden. But then he came to something that surprised him. Written in the book were the words, "But the nightingale is the best of all."

"What?" said the emperor. "The nightingale? I've never heard of it. Yet it lives in my own garden! Must I learn such a thing from a book?"

He called his chief minister, who was so grand that when anyone of lower rank dared to speak with him or ask him a question, he would only answer "Puh!" And that meant nothing at all.

78

"It says here that there is a marvelous bird called a nightingale," said the emperor. "And it seems this bird is the greatest treasure in my empire. Why hasn't anyone ever told me about it?"

"I've never heard of it before," said the chief minister. "It certainly has never sang at court."

"I want it to come and sing for me this evening!" said the emperor. "The whole world knows more than I do about my most valuable possession!"

"I've never heard of it before," repeated the chief minister, "but I will search for and find it."

But where was this bird to be found? The chief minister ran upstairs and downstairs through the rooms and hallways, but no one he asked had ever heard of the nightingale. So he ran back to the emperor and said, "Your Imperial Majesty should not believe everything you read. Most of the things in books are pure invention."

"But this book," said the emperor, "Was sent to me by the mighty emperor of Japan. So it cannot be untrue. I want to hear the nightingale. It must come and sing tonight. If it does not, then the whole court will be whipped right after supper!"

"Tsing-pe!" said the minister, and off he ran, upstairs and downstairs, through rooms and hallways. And half the court ran with him, because they did not want to be whipped. They all kept asking about the nightingale that the whole world knew about except the people at court.

At last, they found a poor little girl in the kitchen who said, "The nightingale? I know her very well! She sings so beautifully! Every evening, I am allowed to take a few table scraps to my poor sick mother who lives by the sea. On my way back, I often rest in the forest and listen to her sing. It brings tears to my eyes, as if my mother were kissing me."

"Little kitchen maid," said the chief minister, "I will find you a good position in the kitchen. You will even be allowed to watch the emperor dine. Just take us to the nightingale right away, for she is expected to sing at court tonight."

So they all set off for the woods, where the nightingale often sang. Half the court came along with the kitchen maid and the chief minister. As they walked along, they heard a cow moo.

"Oh!" said the courtiers, "There it is. It certainly has a powerful voice for such a small animal."

"No, that is a cow mooing," said the little kitchen maid. "We still have a long way to go."

Then the frogs in the pond began to croak. "How delightful!" said the court chaplain. "I can hear her. She sounds like little church bells."

"No, those are frogs," said the little kitchen maid. "But we may hear her any time now."

And then the nightingale began to sing. "There she is," said the kitchen maid. "Listen!" And she pointed to a little gray bird sitting in a tree.

"Is it possible?" asked the chief minister. "I would never have dreamed that a nightingale would look so drab. She must have lost her color at the sight of so many important people."

"My little nightingale," called out the kitchen maid, "Our gracious emperor wishes you to sing for him."

"With great pleasure," replied the nightingale, and the bird began singing in her most beautiful way.

"It sounds like little crystal bells!" said the chief minister. "And look at the way her throat moves. It is strange that we have never heard of her. She will be a great success at court."

"Shall I sing once more for the emperor?" asked the nightingale, for she thought the emperor was among the crowd.

"Excellent nightingale," said the chief minister, "I have the honor of inviting you to court tonight. His majesty will be delighted to enjoy the sweetness of your song."

"My song sounds far better among the green trees," said the nightingale. But she agreed willingly to go with them when she found out that the emperor wished to meet her.

At the palace, every room was polished for the occasion. The fine porcelain walls and floors shined in the light of a thousand gold lamps. The rooms and hallways were full of flowers, and the bells were set tinkling so you couldn't hear a word anyone said.

A golden perch for the nightingale was placed next to the emperor's throne. The whole court was there, and the little kitchen maid had permission to stand beside the door. She now had been given the title of Imperial Kitchen Maid. Everyone was dressed in their finest clothes, and they were all looking at the little gray bird. The emperor nodded at her as a signal to begin.

The nightingale sang so sweetly that tears came to the emperor's eyes and rolled down his cheeks. And then the nightingale's song became even lovelier and her song touched the hearts of all who heard her. The emperor was so pleased that he wanted to hang his golden slippers around her neck. But the nightingale thanked him and said she could not accept his offer, for she had already been rewarded.

"I have seen tears in the emperor's eyes," she said, "and that is the greatest reward of all. I feel honored." And then she sang another song.

"That nightingale's song is simply exquisite," said the ladies of the court. Then they tried to imitate the

sound by keeping water in their throats, trying to warble themselves whenever anyone spoke to them. They wanted to be nightingales, too! Even the servants and chambermaids approved of the nightingale's song. And that is really saying something, because they are always the most difficult to please.

The nightingale was a great success at court. She was to live there and have her own cage. And she had permission to take two flights in the daytime and one

at night. She was escorted by twelve attendants, and each one held on tightly to a silk ribbon attached to her foot. This wasn't any fun for the nightingale!

The whole city was talking about the bird. When people met in the street, one would say, "night" and the other, "gale," and they would understand each other perfectly. Eleven merchants named their children Nightingale, though none of them could sing.

One day a large package arrived with the word "Nightingale" written on it. "Another book about our nightingale!" said the emperor. But it was not a book. It was a little mechanical nightingale. It looked like the real one, but it was made out of beautiful shining gold. When you wound it up, it sang one of the songs the real nightingale sang. Its tail moved up and down, glittering in the light. With the bird came a ribbon on which was written, "The emperor of Japan's nightingale is poor next to the Emperor of China's."

"How delightful!" said everyone, and the man who delivered it was given the title of Imperial Nightingale Supplier.

"Now the two birds must sing together!" said the courtiers. But the duet was not a success. The real bird sang in her own way, and the mechanical one obeyed the clockwork inside it.

"But the mechanical bird is superior," said the imperial music master. "It keeps perfect time."

So the mechanical bird was allowed to sing alone. It sang just as well as the real nightingale and was prettier to look at. Thirty-three times it sang the same

song, without showing a sign of weariness. Everyone would have liked to hear it again. But the emperor decided he wanted to hear another song from the real nightingale. But where was she? No one had noticed when she flew out through the open windows to return to her own green forest.

"What is the meaning of this?" asked the emperor. The courtiers said she was an ungrateful creature.

"We still have the best bird," they said, and the mechanical bird sang once more. It was the thirty-fourth time they heard the same song, but they weren't bored, because it was such a complicated melody.

The imperial music master also praised the mechanical bird highly. He declared it was better than the real nightingale. "You see, Your Majesty, with a real bird, you never know what is coming. But with the mechanical bird, everything is predictable. You can open up the mechanical bird and see how it is made—where the wheels lie, how they move, and how one note follows the other. . ."

"That's exactly what *I* think," agreed everybody. And the imperial music master was given permission to show the bird to the people the next Sunday.

"They, too, should hear it sing," said the emperor. And when they did, the crowd raised their arms in the air and cheered, "Ohh!"

Only one of the fishermen, who had heard the real nightingale, said, "Yes, it sings well, almost like the real one. Yet there is something missing."

The real nightingale was forbidden to return to the empire. The mechanical bird had the honor of a seat on a silken cushion beside the emperor's bed. All

around it lay gifts of gold and precious stones that it had received. The bird was given the title of Grand Imperial Night Table Singer. And it was always placed just to the left of the emperor. You see, the emperor thought the left side was more important because that's where the heart is. Even an emperor's heart is on the left!

The imperial music master wrote a book in twenty-five volumes about the mechanical nightingale. Each one was heavy and learned and full of the most difficult Chinese words. Everyone said they had read and enjoyed the volumes. Otherwise, they would have been considered stupid and they might have been whipped.

A year passed in this way. The emperor, the courtiers, and all the people in China knew every note of the nightingale's song by heart. And for that reason, they appreciated the mechanical bird more than ever. Now they could join in when the bird sang. And they did. Even the street urchins knew the tunes, and the emperor himself could often be heard humming one of the songs.

But one evening, while the mechanical bird was singing and the emperor was lying in bed listening, something went "Clank!" inside the bird. The wheels whirred around very fast for a moment, and then the music came to a sudden stop.

The emperor jumped out of bed and called his personal physician. But what good could a doctor do? Then a clockmaker was sent for, and after a long examination he managed, more or less, to mend the bird. But he said that the wheels were almost worn out. They were impossible to replace, so the bird could not be allowed to sing so often.

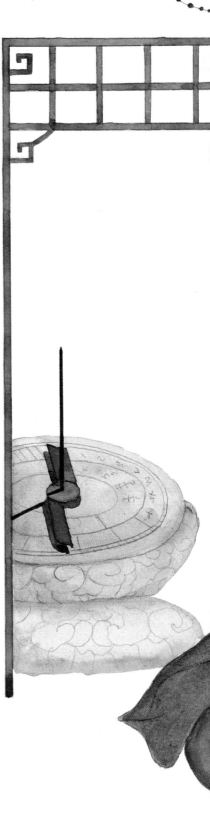

There was a great sadness in the empire. The mechanical nightingale was allowed to sing only once each year, and it sang with great difficulty.

On each of these occasions, the imperial music master made a speech, assuring everyone that the mechanical bird's singing was as good as ever. And then, of course, it *was* as good as ever.

Five years passed, and then a great tragedy struck the country. The emperor fell sick, and everyone agreed he would not live. Although a new emperor

had already been chosen, the people still crowded the streets and asked the chief minister how the old emperor was. But the minister only shook his head and replied, "Puh!"

Cold and pale, the emperor lay on his golden bed. The courtiers thought he was already dead, and they went to pay their respects to the new emperor. The councillors left the palace to discuss the situation, and the servants and chambermaids gathered in little groups to consider the matter over tea and cakes. In the rooms and corridors, thick carpets had been laid to deaden every noise. The whole palace was silent.

But the emperor was not yet dead. As he lay still and pale in bed, the moon shined through the window and lit up his face and the mechanical bird beside him. The poor emperor could scarcely breathe: he felt a great weight on his chest. He opened his eyes and saw Death in the room! He had put on the emperor's golden crown. In one hand, he held the imperial sword and in the other, the splendid imperial banner. Strange figures were clustered all around. These were all the good and bad deeds of the emperor, and they now stood before him, while Death reached for his heart!

"Do you remember me?" they whispered, first one and then another. "Do you remember us?" they went on until a cold sweat formed on the emperor's forehead.

"No! I don't remember!" the emperor cried. "Music, music! Play the great Chinese drum! I do not want to hear what these creatures are saying!"

But they went on and on, and Death, in the Chinese fashion, kept nodding his head at every word.

"Music, music!" shouted the emperor. "Little nightingale, sing!" commanded the emperor. "I beg you, sing! I have given you gold and precious stones. Sing, I beg you, sing!"

But the mechanical bird was silent. There was no one there to wind it up, and so it could not sing. Death stared on at the emperor with his great hollow eyes.

Then suddenly, there came through the window the most beautiful music! It was the real nightingale, sitting on a branch outside the emperor's window. She had heard of the emperor's suffering and had come to sing songs of comfort and hope.

As she sang, the ghostly figures began to fade, and blood quickened its flow through the emperor's weak body. Even Death himself listened to the song, and said, "Go on, little nightingale, don't stop."

"Will you give me the golden sword?" she asked. And then, "Will you give me the imperial banner? Will you give me the emperor's crown?"

Death gave up a treasure for every song the nightingale sang, and still she went on singing. She sang of the peaceful graveyard where white roses bloom and elder trees grow, where the fresh grass is wet with the tears of those left behind.

Then Death was filled with longing to see his own garden again, and he slipped away out the open window like a cold white mist.

"Thank you, thank you!" cried the emperor. "Little bird, I owe you so much. I banished you from

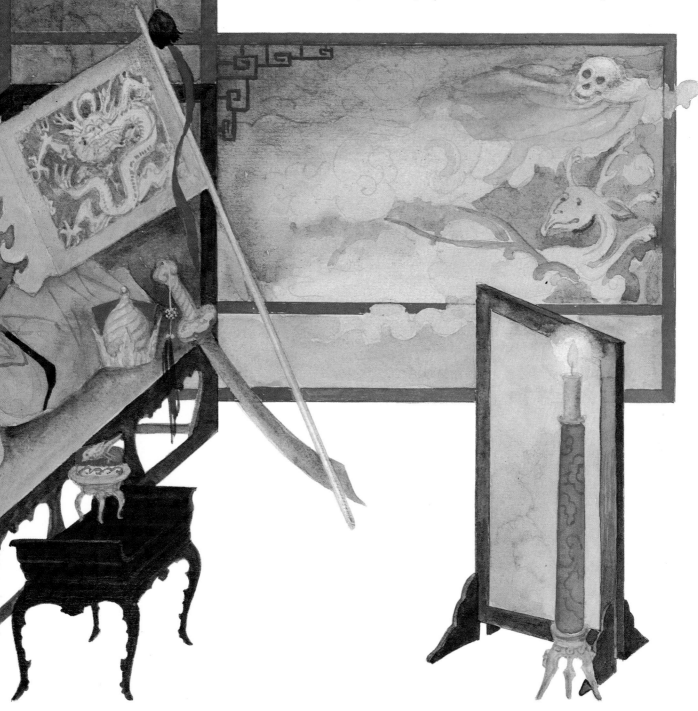

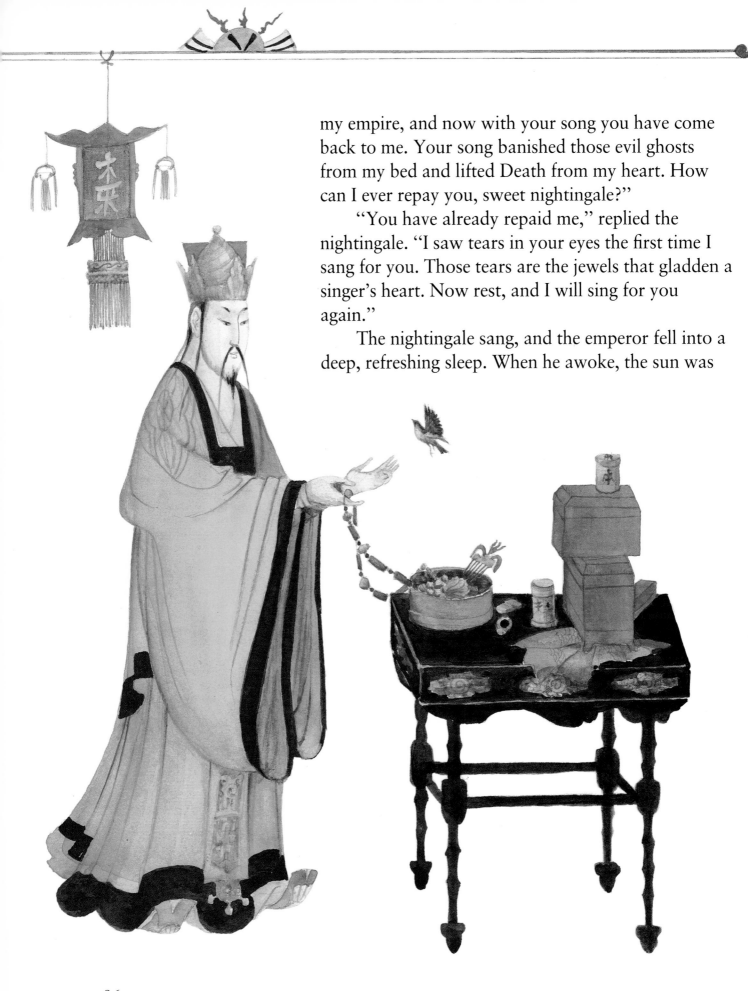

my empire, and now with your song you have come back to me. Your song banished those evil ghosts from my bed and lifted Death from my heart. How can I ever repay you, sweet nightingale?"

"You have already repaid me," replied the nightingale. "I saw tears in your eyes the first time I sang for you. Those tears are the jewels that gladden a singer's heart. Now rest, and I will sing for you again."

The nightingale sang, and the emperor fell into a deep, refreshing sleep. When he awoke, the sun was shining, and he was well. None of the servants had come back yet, for they all thought he was dead. But the nightingale stayed nearby and sang.

"You must stay with me always!" said the emperor. "You shall sing only when you want to, and I will break the mechanical bird into a thousand pieces."

"Don't do that," said the nightingale. "It has done the best it could. Take care of it. I cannot live in the palace, but let me come here whenever I want to."

"In the evenings, I will sit on a branch outside your window and sing songs that will make you happy and wise. I will sing to you about people who are happy and people who suffer. And I will sing about the good and evil all around you. For a songbird flies everywhere—to the poor peasant's cottage and the fisherman's hut—and it knows people far from your palace and your court."

"I love your heart more than I love your crown, yet the crown has something holy about it. So I will come and sing for you. But you must promise me one thing."

"Whatever you wish," said the emperor. He had put on his imperial robes, and now he stood upright, holding his gold sword against his heart.

"I ask you this: let no one know you have a little bird who tells you everything. Then all will go well." With those words, the nightingale flew away.

Later, the servants came in to look at their dead emperor. They stood there, amazed, when the emperor said, "Good morning!"

The Princess and the Pea

Once upon a time there was a prince who wanted to marry a princess, but she had to be a true princess. He traveled all over the world looking for one, and he met plenty of princesses. But there was always something wrong with them. He was never quite sure they were true princesses. There was always some doubt. So the prince returned home tired and sad. He had so wanted a real princess!

Then one night there was a terrible storm. There was thunder and lightning, and the rain poured down: it was awful! Suddenly there was a knock at the castle door, and the old king went to open it. It was a princess—and what a sorry sight she was! The rain was running down her hair and clothes, and water poured in the tips of her shoes and out again at the heel. Yet, she said she was a real princess.

"We shall soon see about that!" thought the old queen. She didn't say anything, but she slipped into the bedroom, took all the linens off the bed, and placed a pea on the bare mattress. Then she laid twenty mattresses on top of the pea and twenty feather beds on top of the mattresses. That was where the princess had to spend the night.

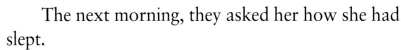

The next morning, they asked her how she had slept.

"Horribly!" the princess complained. "I couldn't sleep a wink. God knows what was in that bed, but it made me completely black and blue. It was awful!"

And then they knew that she was a true princess, because she had felt the pea through twenty mattresses and twenty feather beds. No one but a real princess could have such sensitive, tender skin!

So the prince married her, for he was sure at last that he had found a real princess. The pea was placed in the Royal Museum, and you can see it there still, unless it has been stolen.

Now that's a real story!